# Believe No Evil

# Believe No Evil

## JANE EDWARDS

**Thorndike Press • Chivers Press**
**Thorndike, Maine, USA   Bath, England**

This Large Print edition is published by Thorndike Press, USA and by Chivers Press, England.

Published in 2000 in the U.K. by arrangement with Jane Edwards

Published in 2000 in the U.S. by arrangement with Jane Edwards

U.S.  Hardcover  0-7862-2843-1  (Candlelight Series Edition)
U.K.  Hardcover  0-7540-4374-6  (Chivers Large Print)

The text of this Large Print edition is unabridged.
Other aspects of the book may vary from the original edition.

Set in 16 pt. Plantin.

Printed in the United States on permanent paper.

**British Library Cataloguing in Publication Data available**

**Library of Congress Cataloging-in-Publication Data**

Edwards, Jane (Jane Campbell), 1932–
    Believe no evil / Jane Edwards.
        p.  cm.
    ISBN 0-7862-2843-1 (lg. print : hc : alk. paper)
    1. San Francisco (Calif.) — Fiction.  2. Large type books.
I. Title.
PS3555.D933 B45    2000
  813'.54—dc21
                                                      00-059375

*For a delightful aunt and uncle,*

VERN AND STEVE CAMPBELL

# Chapter One

"I simply don't know. I had hoped that you could help me decide —"

Jennifer Sheldon's voice trailed off uncertainly. She had never felt so tongue-tied. It sounded ridiculous to say that she was searching for something but wouldn't know what it was until she had found it.

With an impatient gesture, she rumpled her smooth, short cap of black hair. Her dark eyebrows seemed to tilt upward even more questioningly than usual, and distress was mirrored in her wide blue eyes.

Miss Lasky, the school's vocational counselor, shook her head. "I'm here to offer you guidance, Jennifer, but I can't very well choose a career for you. With your experience, you could qualify as a full-fledged librarian at graduation. Or teaching might be the answer." She snapped the file shut, and held out her hand. "It's up to you, my dear. Give the matter some further thought this summer, then come to see me again next fall. Good luck!"

"Thank you."

Slowly Jenny turned to leave the office. How absurd, she thought, to be twenty years old and still not know what she wanted to do with her life. She had always loved books; three years ago she had entered Kingston College with the intention of becoming a librarian. In time, though, she had grown more and more dissatisfied with her choice. She wanted to live life, not just read about it!

And there was only one year left. In September she would be a senior. She had to make a decision soon.

She emerged from the building, a small neat girl with a troubled face, and turned toward the inner Quad. Like many lanes on campus, the path was shaded by rustling palm trees that cast their spiky shadows across benches perched in their shelter.

A bright auburn head, which had been bent over the pages of a manuscript, bobbed up at her approach. "That didn't take long," Fran Clarke commented. "Any new suggestions?"

"No. I guess it's something I'll have to figure out for myself." Jenny dropped down on the bench, peering at the dog-eared script in her friend's hand. "Golly, I envy you," she sighed. "You're so — single-minded."

"About acting? It's all I ever wanted to do," Fran said simply. "Besides, the theatre is a solid tradition in our family. My grandparents helped kill vaudeville, and Dad and Mother practically grew up on stage. Having this chance to do summer stock with the Little Theatre is like a dream come true for me."

"It sounds wonderful." Jenny gathered up her books again, wishing that she, too, had some lifelong ambition that she could look forward to achieving.

The two girls started leisurely across the Quad, skirting a high hedge of oleanders that fringed the library.

Fran glanced up at the somber brick facade of the building. "Are you going to stay on here during the summer?"

"I suppose so. What with vacation classes going ahead nonstop, there'll be plenty of need for librarians. It sort of depends on Mark," Jenny added. "If he can get home on leave, I'd like to spend part of the time with him."

"He still hasn't written. That doesn't sound like Mark."

"No. It's — it's odd." A tiny line puckered between Jenny's eyebrows. She tried to laugh away the seed of worry.

"I showed you those funny little post-cards he sent me from Japan, didn't I? Just a line or two scrawled on each one to let me know he hadn't gone over to the Marines or the Green Berets, or something."

"As if he would — after graduating from Annapolis!" Fran giggled, then quickly sobered. "Don't fret about him. He and the rest of the Navy are probably just out on maneuvers."

Jenny nodded uneasily, her frown deepening. Her brother was stationed on a destroyer in the Pacific, but this fact had never prevented him from writing her frequently in the past. Yet it was almost three weeks now since she had received one of his letters, or even a hasty postcard. It was more than odd, she thought. It was downright peculiar!

She and Fran moved politely aside, making room on the narrow path for a group of alumni. With final exams over and only a few days of school remaining, parents who had come down to see the graduation or to enroll new students for the fall semester seemed to be everywhere.

Wistfully, Jenny watched them pass. Her own parents had died in a boating accident while she was still in high school. Mark, a brand-new naval officer at the time, had done everything he could to ease her sorrow, and had arranged with generous neighbors to take her into their home. When she was awarded the scholarship to Kingston College, no brother could possibly have been prouder than he. And, no matter how many thousands of miles he traveled, Mark had always kept in touch with her by mail at least once a week.

That was why she found his sudden silence so puzzling. She couldn't help worrying that he might be sick or wounded, although common sense told her that if that were the case, she would have been notified. But what other reason could there possibly be?

"Jenny!"

A voice broke into her troubled thoughts. Debra Tucker, a plump, pretty girl with an amiable but scatterbrained disposition, hurried down the dorm steps toward them.

"Aloha!" called Fran and Jenny in unison.

Debra's smile widened. "Isn't that just the prettiest word you ever did hear?" she exclaimed in her soft Southern drawl. "I've been practicing it ever since my Mamma and Daddy made our reservations on the Princess Kaiulani. It's hard to believe that Thursday is actually sailing day."

"Well, I can believe it," Fran laughed. "We've been hearing about nothing but that trip to Hawaii for months!"

"Pay no attention to her, Deb," Jenny said staunchly. "I know you're going to enjoy every minute of the tour."

"I surely do hope so. That is, if we don't get attacked by pirates!" Debra added with a shiver of excitement.

Fran rolled her eyes heavenward. "Pirates! That was two hundred years ago, you silly goose!"

"Oh, for land's sake, everyone knows that," Debra scoffed. "I'm talking about the modern kind. Don't you girls ever read the papers? There have been two or three ships halted, and their cargoes stolen, just recently. And it happened right off the coast of California!"

"Come to think of it, I do recall reading something about that," Jenny admitted. She wrinkled her brow, trying to remember the details of the news item.

Fran, however, refused to take the matter seriously. "Then, I advise you to bone up on what the skull and crossbones look like, so you'll be prepared. Incidentally, if you're held for ransom be sure to telegraph Mrs. Ogilvie. You know how fussy she is about always knowing where we girls are going."

"Mrs. Ogilvie!" Debra clapped her hand to her forehead. "Oh, good grief, Jenny, she sent me out here to get you. I plumb forgot, what with all this silly chatter about pirates. You'd better hurry right on in."

Jenny scampered up the stairs, wondering what it was that their housemother wanted. It must be something fairly important for her to have dispatched another girl with a message.

Hastening inside, she quickly crossed the foyer, but before she had reached the small office alongside the stairway, Mrs. Ogilvie stepped out to meet her. She was a large, usually placid woman of early middle age. At the moment, however, she appeared to be a bit distraught.

"You have company, Jenny," she said. "They're waiting for you in the parlor."

Jenny's heart gave a leap of joyful relief. Mark! So this was why he hadn't written. He had planned a surprise visit!

Excitedly, she whirled toward the parlor, then paused, bewildered. "Did you say *they* are waiting?"

"Yes, dear. Two men," Mrs. Ogilvie

announced. Something about the house-mother's tense expression should have warned her, Jenny thought later. But nothing could really have prepared her for the visitors who awaited her. Crossing the threshold into the parlor, she halted in blank surprise.

Two men rose and started forward. Astonished, Jenny stared at their neat white uniforms, at the businesslike side arms buckled around their waists, at their armbands stenciled with the insignia "S.P."

S.P. — which stood for Shore Patrol.

Jenny stiffened in terror. Mark, she thought. Something dreadful must have happened to Mark!

# Chapter Two

"Miss Jennifer Sheldon?" asked one of the Shore Patrolmen.

Jenny nodded mutely. A cold hard knot of fear tightened in her throat. If only they didn't look so *grim!*

"Please come in and sit down," the second man suggested, not unkindly. "Perhaps it would be better if we closed the door."

Suddenly it seemed to Jenny that she was reliving an old tragic scene. Several years before, a pair of police officers had arrived with the news that her parents had been drowned. The faces of these men had the same grave look. Had they come on a similar errand?

Somehow she forced her quavering legs to carry her to one of the stiff straight-backed chairs near the center of the room. She sank down, grateful for its support.

"It's — it's about my brother, isn't it?" she whispered, clenching her hands rigidly in her lap. "Has he been injured? Or — ?"

They hastened to reassure her. "Please

don't look so frightened, Miss Sheldon," said the man who appeared to be in charge. "To the best of our knowledge, your brother is perfectly all right."

Jenny drew a shaky breath, feeling the giddy sensation recede. She had never come so close to fainting in her entire life.

"Oh, thank goodness," she murmured. "I was so afraid —"

"However," the man continued, "our visit does concern Lieutenant Sheldon. When did you last hear from him?"

"Nearly three weeks ago," Jenny replied. "The postcards he mailed from Japan were the last news I received from Mark. I'm expecting a letter any day now."

The men exchanged guarded glances. "Have you seen him recently?" they persisted.

"Not for over a year."

Jenny's courage had returned, and with it the persistent twinge of worry that she had been unable to dismiss. She faced the men squarely.

"Please tell me why you are here," she said. "I've been rather concerned about not having heard from my brother. He — he's all the family I have left."

"I'm sorry. We're only following orders,

you understand," the Shore Patrolman explained. "A few days ago our San Diego base received a bulletin informing us that your brother had jumped ship in San Francisco. Subsequently, a young naval officer answering his description was involved in a waterfront brawl in that city."

"Oh, no!" Jenny gasped. "There must be some mistake!"

"I'm afraid not. His ship sailed without him. Lieutenant Sheldon has been officially listed as AWOL. You have no clue as to his present whereabouts?"

"Of course not!"

Even as she flung the words at them, Jenny was battling down her indignation. These men were only doing their duty. They didn't know Mark as she did.

She tried to make them understand. "My brother would never do anything to discredit his uniform. He loves the Navy! If Mark is missing, there must be some other explanation. He's no deserter!"

"I hope you're right, miss," the Shore Patrolman said uncomfortably. He looked as if he admired her for her loyalty.

Nevertheless, Jenny could tell that he was not convinced. The evidence against Mark must be very black indeed.

Fear came rushing back as the door

clicked shut behind them. "Jumped ship . . . waterfront brawl. . . . AWOL. . . ." The ominous words buzzed round and round, like a swarm of angry bees in Jenny's brain. At first, she told herself that they had identified the wrong man. Perhaps there was someone who closely resembled her brother. But in that case —

Jenny got unsteadily to her feet. In that case, where was Mark?

A faint clatter of dishes and silverware from the dining room reached Jenny's ears when she stepped back into the hall. Her appetite had vanished, though; she paid no attention to the sounds. Instead, she walked out the front door and down the steps. The brisk evening air tingled against her skin. With hands thrust deep into her pockets, she turned into the empty street. Not until she had gone a block or more did she make an effort to sort out her jumbled thoughts.

Mark was missing. His ship had put out to sea without him. That much was concrete, Jenny decided, since the Navy would have no cause to lie. She felt less certain about the brawl, however. Although he could never have been called a sissy, Mark was a peaceful sort of person who had never cared much for fighting.

"It just doesn't make sense!"

Without realizing it, Jenny had spoken the words aloud. An approaching freshman gave her a startled look before hurrying past. Intent on the perplexing problem, she hardly noticed him. She walked on, puzzling over the enigma of Mark's disappearance. But an hour later the solution was no plainer than when she had left the dorm.

A glance at her wristwatch brought her aimless wandering to a halt. It was after six o'clock, well past the time when she should have reported for duty at the library. Jenny had never considered the three-hour evening stint much of a chore before, but tonight she regarded the prospect with misgivings. How could she possibly concentrate on her job at a time like this?

Yet as she paused, undecided, she realized that by now the dorm must be buzzing with questions — questions to which she could give no answer. She was too heartsick and worried to feel like confiding in any of her friends. Maybe by tomorrow —

Reluctantly, she cut across the Quad to the library. It was still quiet so early after dinner. With dogged determination, Jenny set to work replacing returned books in the stacks. She forced herself to sort the titles correctly — fiction, nonfiction, volumes for the research room. Somehow the hours dragged past.

Most of the students had left by eight-thirty, when the door to the main reading room was flung open and a short, rotund figure strode up to the desk. In spite of her despondent frame of mind, Jenny smiled wanly at the sight of Professor Avery's armload of books.

"Good evening, sir," she said, helping him unload the books onto the counter.

"Ah, Jenny, I'm glad it's you." He chuckled. "My good sister Ursula finally shamed me into cleaning out my study. Imagine my horror when I discovered this — this conglomeration of volumes, each of which, I fear, is sadly overdue. Another librarian would have reported me for grand larceny!"

Jenny was appalled to find that some of the due dates were six months delinquent. "And so should I," she scolded him. "Honestly, Dr. Avery, you're supposed to set a good example for the students!"

Clement Avery bobbed his snow-white mane in contrite agreement. "And for my grandson now, also," he admitted.

For the first time, Jenny noticed the

small boy standing shyly behind the professor. The child's face was pale beneath its shock of corn-silk hair. His large intelligent brown eyes peered unblinkingly back at her.

"This is my grandson, Paul," Dr. Avery proudly introduced him. "Paul, I want you to meet Miss Jenny Sheldon. Not only is she one of my brightest students but something of a good fairy as well. She is going to protect me from that terrible dragon, the head librarian!"

Paul gazed suspiciously around the room. On spying no one who resembled a dragon, he held out his hand to Jenny. "How do you do?" he said. "Have you any books about Australia?"

She nodded. "Yes, several. Shall I find some for you?"

Jenny located two simply written books and an atlas of maps depicting the island continent. Paul grasped them eagerly. She seated him at a little table where he could study them in comfort, then returned to the check-out desk.

Dr. Avery told her something about the child while she totaled up the fines for the overdue books.

"Poor lad, his mother died in an automobile crash last year," the professor confided. "Since then, he has been living with an aunt back East. She and her husband are expecting a new baby soon, however, so Ursula and I offered to keep Paul with us for the summer."

"He looks like a lively youngster," Jenny remarked, hoping that the care of a little boy would not prove to be too taxing for the professor and his sister, who were both in their sixties. "What about his father?"

"My son is a geologist, working with an oil company in Australia," he explained. "His contract will be up in September. At that time he and Paul will be permanently reunited. Meanwhile, we are doing the best we can for the child."

Jenny had heard rumors that Dr. Avery, who was head of the Languages Department, would be absent from the campus during the summer.

"Now that vacation is almost here, you ought to have plenty of time to get acquainted with him." She smiled.

The professor paid his fine, but it was obvious that the concerned expression that crossed his face had nothing to do with overdue books.

"Unfortunately, I had already made other plans for the summer some months ago," he sighed. "When one of the directors of a new, charitable foundation in northern California asked me to assist in the teaching of Oriental Languages there, I could not refuse. Do you know anything about the Center for International Understanding and Cooperation?"

Jenny shook her head.

Dr. Avery did not seem surprised. "Few people do, as yet," he said. "The Center's work is very similar to that of the Peace Corps. Although the program has been in existence for little more than a year, it has already done much to aid several needy countries. Its aim is to help the citizens of these Asiatic nations to develop their own resources, both of manpower and of material. If this can be accomplished, we will have won a vital battle in the fight against hunger."

Over the past year the economic decline in Asia had caused world-wide alarm.

"Good for you," Jenny said. "But I don't understand what a professor of languages can do to help."

"A number of unselfish young Americans have volunteered to spend two years abroad. Together with well-educated natives, they will act as leaders in what the Center terms 'Operation Bootstrap.' However, they can accomplish very little without at least a rudimentary knowledge of the language of the country where they will be working," Dr. Avery explained. "It will be my task to tutor these young men and women — teach them as much as possible in a few short weeks."

He glanced anxiously at his small grandson. "I gladly offered to donate my time to this cause. But I fear it will mean a quiet, probably even dull summer for Paul."

"What a shame! Are he and Miss Ursula going with you?" Jenny asked.

"Yes, of course. One of the close friends I made during my years in the Far East was a shipping magnate named Hammond Marsh," Dr. Avery went on. "Since his retirement from business, he has become one of the Center's main sponsors. He is an extremely wealthy man, who owns a considerable amount of property in Monterey. Hammond writes that he is placing a comfortable house at my disposal during our stay there."

A "comfortable house" in the lovely seacoast town would probably represent quite a change from the cozy bungalow in which the Averys now lived, thought Jenny. More than once, she and her classmates had been entertained at the delightfully unpretentious teas given by the widowed professor and his sister. Miss Ursula was an excellent housekeeper and a wonderful cook, but there was just so much that any one person could do. Then, too, Jenny had noticed that lately the elderly woman seemed to be troubled by arthritis.

Dr. Avery appeared to read her thoughts.

"A large strange house and a mischievous little boy," he murmured. "Ursula's health is not up to such a strain. As for myself — I shudder at the prospect of that long drive."

He leaned heavily against the counter. "Perhaps you could help me, Jenny. Do you know of any student who would be willing to share the driving in exchange for a ride north? I should also like to find a responsible girl to live with us for a few months — someone who could look after Paul and be of help to my sister."

Jenny drew her dark brows together in thoughtful concentration. "I wish I did," she answered after a moment. "Many of the students here at Kingston are from the Bay Area, so it should be easy enough to find someone who needs transportation. The other problem will be harder to solve. Most of the girls I know already have plans for the summer."

She promised to inquire among her friends, however, and to let him know if she learned of anyone who could provide the answer to his dilemma.

"I'd appreciate that." Dr. Avery beckoned to Paul, who trudged up to return the books he had borrowed. "We will be leaving on Monday, so that leaves only a few days to locate someone," the professor added as he turned toward the door. "Enjoy your vacation, and don't worry about our little problems, my dear."

In spite of this advice, Jenny couldn't help feeling concerned. Dr. Avery was a darling; but, competent as he was in his own profession, she doubted that he would be able to cope with road maps and traffic hazards.

She had first met the professor several semesters ago when she had enrolled in one of his courses in Japanese. At that time it had seemed likely that Mark would be based near Tokyo for a year or two, and she had looked forward to visiting him there. But it hadn't worked out that way. Since then, her brother's ship had taken him all over the Pacific, and although she had learned a great deal about the Japanese language, she had never had a chance to make any practical use of the knowledge.

Thinking about Mark brought her own problem sharply back into focus. Tears welled in her eyes. If only he would write — at least let her know that he was alive!

It suddenly occurred to her that he could be a victim of amnesia. A blow on the head sometimes caused that to happen. He could be anywhere by now, she thought miserably — and he mightn't even remember who he was!

Night had clamped down on the campus by the time she left the library. Jenny rounded the hedge of oleanders and started up the familiar path, feeling vaguely light-headed. Belatedly, she recalled that she had had nothing to eat since lunch time. She was still too depressed to have much of an appetite, but logic reminded her that it would do Mark no good if she were to become ill.

Someday soon he might need her help!

She quickened her footsteps, wondering for the dozenth time what lay behind his strange disappearance. As she did so, she heard a faint scrunch of gravel behind her. There was something stealthy about the sound.

Almost immediately Jenny dismissed the thought as nonsense. Why should anyone be skulking here, on the outskirts of the

Quad? Nevertheless, she walked a little faster. Street lights on campus were all but nonexistent, and the closest buildings stood dark and empty.

Once again her ears picked up the furtive rattle of pebbles. This time, Jenny could not resist the impulse to glance back over her shoulder. Something moved in the shadows behind her, something that was instantly swallowed up in the dense foliage adjoining the path. But in that split second Jenny glimpsed a flash of white cloth.

Anger quickly replaced the rush of fear that had welled within her. Only a few hours earlier she had been confronted by two men wearing white uniforms. She had told the Shore Patrolmen the truth — that she knew nothing about Mark's whereabouts. Now it seemed they hadn't believed her!

Humiliation brought a blush of fury surging to her cheeks. The notion that she was being constantly watched, trailed wherever she went, was almost too much for Jenny to bear. She had no proof that it was one of the Navy's policemen who had darted into the shrubbery just then, but there was little doubt in her mind. Apparently, they expected her to lead them to Mark!

Hunger forgotten, Jenny sprinted the rest of the distance to the dorm, pounded up the steps, and slammed the front door. There was no one in the hall; she fled blindly to her room and hurled herself onto the bed.

Supposing Mark didn't return, Jenny thought wildly, sobbing into her pillow. She might never see him again! What was she to do?

After a few minutes, though, reason returned. Trust and loyalty banished the frightening doubts that had leaped into her mind. She sat up, groping for a handkerchief. Mark was all right, she told herself fiercely. She had to keep on believing that!

The next two days seemed to pass in slow motion. Jenny was relieved that Mrs. Ogilvie had mentioned nothing to the other girls about her two alarming visitors. Questions were avoided, and she was able to wave good-bye to her friends with a pretense of cheerfulness.

Fran left Friday evening; by Saturday, even Debra was gone amid a chorus of bon voyages and alohas that threatened to echo throughout the corridors for hours afterward.

Feeling terribly alone, Jenny wandered

into the main hall that afternoon to await the arrival of the mail. Sooner or later, she thought hopefully, there was bound to be word from Mark. He couldn't keep her in suspense forever!

But there wasn't even a scrap of advertising for her among the sheaf of envelopes delivered by the mailman. Her spirits sagged as she riffled through them a second time. Not until then did she glance at the small parcel that had arrived with the letters.

At first, Jenny couldn't believe her eyes. Then her heart gave a jubilant leap as she recognized her brother's familiar handwriting.

She knew that Mark wouldn't let her down. But why a package?

With trembling fingers, she tore off the brown outer wrapping, and fumbled at the lid of the box. A wad of crumpled tissue paper protected the contents from breakage. Pulling this aside, Jenny lifted out the object Mark had sent her. A look of absolute bewilderment came over her face.

It was a tiny, exquisitely carved statuette.

# Chapter Three

At any other time, knowing Mark's un-
quenchable sense of humor, Jenny might
have regarded the package as some sort of a
joke. Or, at the most, as an unusual gift.
Under the circumstances, though —

Completely mystified, she rummaged
through the little box, scanning the crumpled wrappings carefully for a note or a
card that might have been enclosed. But
the parcel contained not a word of writing.

Only the statuette.

Sinking down on a chair, she stared for a
long moment at the daintily carved figures
reposing on a seat of wood. They were the
traditional three monkeys of Oriental
legend: see no evil, hear no evil, speak no
evil. The finely detailed image was a thing
of beauty. But aside from its artistic quali-
ties, Jenny couldn't help feeling that Mark
must have had some special purpose in
sending her this particular figurine.

"Surely he knows that I've been worried
sick about him," she murmured.

Then, too, he undoubtedly realized that

the Shore Patrol would have contacted her in an effort to locate him. The lack of a message enclosed with the present must mean that Mark wanted no one, not even her, to know where he was.

But if that were true, why had he sent her the package?

"Think hard!" she prodded herself. "There's some significance attached to the statuette. It represents a clue of some kind."

She turned the delicate object around and around in her hands. The monkeys stared solemnly back at her.

See no evil, hear no evil, speak no evil.

Suddenly Jenny jumped up, scattering papers in all directions.

"That's it!" she cried triumphantly. "If there were a fourth monkey, he would be thinking no evil. That's what Mark is asking of me — to believe no evil!"

In other words, she decided, her brother was telling her to have faith in him. For some reason, he dared not write, but rather than allow her to worry and wonder any longer he had chosen this method of relieving her anxiety.

"He wants me to understand that he is doing nothing wrong," Jenny reflected. "No matter how dreadful the situation looks, I'm to trust him."

And she did. All along she had told herself that Mark could never be involved in anything dishonorable. Just the same, it was a relief to have some reassurance.

Unfortunately, the solution to the riddle of the monkeys posed more questions than ever. Where was Mark, and what was he doing? Could he be working on some secret government mission? A mission so important that only he and a few of his superiors knew of it?

The thought that her brother could be serving his country in a special way made Jenny tingle with pride. But this was only a guess. Even if it were true, it might mean that Mark was in far greater danger than she had previously suspected.

"If only I knew where he is!" she groaned. "Maybe I could help!"

All at once Jenny realized that she had overlooked the most vital clue of all. She dove for the brown paper wrapping, smoothed it out, and squinted to identify the smudged postmark. The round inked imprint surprised her.

"San Francisco! He must have been there all along!"

Her first impulse was to telephone immediately for train or bus reservations.

Then she remembered the blur of white on the path behind her a few nights earlier. It was possible that she had been mistaken, of course. Probably it was only nerves that had caused her to suspect someone was following her. But just in case she hadn't been wrong —

*The Shore Patrol mightn't be the only group looking for Mark,* a warning inner voice cautioned her.

No, Jenny decided, she couldn't take the chance of exposing her brother's secret — whatever it was. She still intended to go to him, if possible. But she must make certain that no unfriendly eyes followed her when she left.

Mark's life might depend on it!

Absentmindedly, Jenny replaced the statuette in its box and gathered up every scrap of wrapping paper. Leaving the rest of the mail on the hall table, she climbed the stairs to her room and tucked Mark's present away in the back of a drawer. Then she walked over to the open window, hoping that the fresh air would clear her brain and help her think of a way out of this predicament.

Any form of public transportation was out, she decided. It would be too easy for others to trace her that way. Besides, what would she do once she arrived in San Francisco? Hotels and restaurants were terribly expensive, and it was a month yet until the next installment of her allowance, set up by a trust fund in her parents' will, would be paid. All she had to live on until then was the small salary she had earned by working at the library. She didn't even have a car —

Jenny's eyes widened abruptly. But Dr. Avery did! If he hadn't succeeded in finding a girl to help with the driving, her problem might be solved! She herself had encountered no one willing to take on the chore. Perhaps his luck had been no better than hers!

Monterey, she knew, was only a few hours' ride from San Francisco. She would need a place to live while searching for Mark. Realistically, she faced the fact that it might be days, even weeks, before she located her brother. Why couldn't she assist the Averys at the same time?

She darted back down the stairs and cut across campus to the quiet street where most of Kingston's faculty resided.

Jenny was small in stature, but the frail little lady who answered her knock made her seem tall by comparison. There was nothing stinting about Miss Avery's smile, though, when she greeted the girl on the doorstep.

"Why, Jenny! What a pleasant surprise," she exclaimed. "Do come in. The house is a bit topsy-turvy at the moment, but you mustn't mind that. It's just that we haven't been able to decide which possessions to take with us and which to leave behind."

Jenny never failed to marvel at the wonderful knack Miss Ursula had for making people feel welcome. Although everything about her — from her turn-of-the-century hairdo to the scent of lavender sachet that clung to her clothes — was old-fashioned to an extreme, she delighted in the company of young people and thoroughly approved of their modern, independent outlook.

"I'm sorry to disturb you at such a busy time," Jenny apologized. "The other evening Dr. Avery mentioned that he was looking for someone to help with the driving on your trip to Monterey. Do you know if he has found anyone yet?"

"No, dear, he hasn't," Miss Ursula sighed. "Truthfully, the thought of that long drive worries me. Clement is not as vigorous as he was twenty years ago, and details such as highway markers seem to elude him. We may all wind up in Colorado!"

"The professor is worried about you, too," Jenny admitted. "He fears that caring for both Paul and a big house will be a burden for you. I promised to try to locate a girl to help out during the summer months, but there doesn't seem to be anyone available." She paused, wondering how to phrase her request. "Except me, that is," she added. "I'd like to come if it wouldn't be an imposition. Would you mind very much — sharing your home with an outsider?"

"Not at all. In fact," Miss Ursula confided, "I think it's the best idea Clement has had in months! Shall we go tell him the good news now?"

They found Dr. Avery in his study, sorting books into a carton. Jenny's decision seemed to remove a heavy weight from his shoulders. He smiled at her in delight.

"Can you be ready early Monday morning?"

"Yes, indeed," she assured him.

Noticing that Paul was morosely scuffling his feet in a corner of the room, she walked over and gently took his hand.

"Aren't you looking forward to the trip?"

"I won't know anyone up there," the little boy grumbled.

"Neither will I at first," Jenny said. "But I wouldn't be surprised if we made lots of friends before long. While we're waiting for them to get to know us, we could probably find some exciting things to do. Have you ever hunted for seashells, or gone swimming in the ocean?"

He shook his head, but his brown eyes brightened. "Can we really do that? You're not just pretending?"

"Wait and see. We'll have a wonderful time!"

She crossed her heart to seal the promise, then turned back to Dr. Avery to discuss the details of their departure. Before Jenny left, Miss Ursula treated them all to generous servings of Danish pastry and freshly perked coffee.

Jenny lingered only long enough to enjoy the treat and thank her hostess. There were a million things to be done — packing, handing her notice in to the library, persuading Mrs. Ogilvie to store her trunk in the basement of the dorm — and only Sunday was left in which to accomplish them all.

She caught her breath. How quickly unexpected events had taken over her life!

It was hard to believe that by Monday she would have left this peaceful little college town far behind. Five hundred miles to the north, Monterey awaited her.

Monterey — and then what?

Impatiently, Jenny shrugged aside the question.

"I'll face one problem at a time!"

# Chapter Four

The first twenty miles were the hardest. At least that's what Jenny kept telling herself. She still hadn't quite mastered the crotchety gear shift, and several times the wheezing of the clutch had come close to throwing her into a panic. But the wheel remained reassuringly steady beneath her hands, and she had to admit that the ancient black sedan rode comfortably enough.

"I feel rather like Al Capone," she giggled to Dr. Avery. "I'm sure he must have staged his get-aways in a car exactly like this!"

Fortunately for him, she added silently, the old-time gangster had never been forced to cope with the San Diego Freeway. Even though the morning commuter rush was past, the thoroughfare's six lanes were clogged with high-speed traffic. She began to feel the strain of tension after an hour or two of trying to keep up with the rapid flow, and a glance at the dashboard gauge warned her that the engine temperature was rising toward a dangerously high peak.

"I'm afraid this automobile was built for a more leisurely pace," she declared. "Much more of this speed-limit driving will cause the radiator to boil over."

"Perhaps we could find an alternate route," Miss Ursula suggested. "There is really no great hurry. I for one would prefer a chance to slow down and enjoy the scenery."

Jenny flashed her a grateful smile in the rear-view mirror. "Laguna Beach should be coming up soon. We'll swing off the freeway there and ask directions at a service station."

This was easily accomplished. Before long, they were chugging along a winding two-lane road. Graceful stretches of sandy beach arced invitingly a few yards off to their left.

His first glimpse of the Pacific Ocean brought a gleeful reaction from Paul. "It's huge, it's gigantic, it's enormous!" he whooped exuberantly. "I'll bet I could see whales and everything out there!"

With the scorching summer heat still a month or so away, the southern California slopes were green with foliage. Vivid flower gardens bedecked the hilly little towns through which they passed. The tautness within Jenny eased now that they had stopped rushing along at such a breakneck velocity. After days of pointless worrying, it felt wonderful to have a definite goal in mind again.

She glanced at the numbers twirling slowly upward on the speedometer. Each figure that eased into sight brought her a mile closer to Mark!

Miss Ursula had packed a tasty picnic lunch, and shortly after noon Paul pointed out a perfect spot in which to enjoy their informal meal. In a matter of minutes the crisp fried chicken, potato salad, and rolls had disappeared. They lingered beside the placid seashore for a bit longer while Paul played at the edge of the surf, but Jenny's eagerness to be under way soon proved catching.

Somehow, now, the distance didn't seem so great. "I could drive for hours yet," she told Dr. Avery when he made a polite but not very convincing offer to take over the wheel.

It was on the outskirts of Long Beach that she noticed the red Volkswagen for the first time. Like a hundred other cars had done that day, it had followed along behind them for a brief interval, and then had pulled out to pass the slow-moving old sedan. She would have thought no more about it, had Paul not commented on the unusual license plate.

"B-Y-E." He spelled out the first three letters of the old blue and gold plate. "He's telling us good bye!"

"Probably so," Jenny agreed with a laugh. "But no matter how many cars zoom out in front of us, we'll get there just the same."

For the next couple of hours she concentrated on wending her way through the steadily increasing flow of traffic that surged around the sprawling environs of Los Angeles. It was a relief to everyone when they were at last free of the city congestion and breezing along the less heavily traveled coast road again. Even so, Paul was beginning to find the long drive tedious. To distract him, Jenny suggested that they pass the time by playing a game.

"Let's each choose a color and count the number of cars we spot of that particular shade," she said.

Paul eagerly fell in with the idea. "I like red best."

"Good! I'll take green."

". . . twenty-three, twenty-four . . ." Paul's total mounted rapidly. "Twenty — oh, look, Jenny! There's the BYE car again."

Somewhat to her surprise, Jenny saw that he was right. The same red Volkswagen was trundling along in the slow lane, only a few yards in front of them.

"How peculiar," she remarked. "That car passed us hours ago. He should be miles ahead by this time."

Of course, she added to herself, the driver could have stopped for a late lunch. Or been delayed by any of a dozen different things, for that matter.

He didn't seem to be in as much of a hurry now either, she noticed. The little red car was definitely dawdling. She endured the creeping pace for a few moments longer, then coaxed a burst of speed from the ancient sedan and swung around to pass the Volkswagen. As she did so, she caught a glimpse of the other driver. Her fleeting glance took in a thatch of sandy hair and a face that looked purposefully grim. Then she was beyond him and pulling away gradually.

"What does our license plate say?" Paul grinned. Jenny giggled with him. "I don't remember. Maybe we should apply for a BYE, too! Better look for some different red cars. I imagine we've seen the last of that one."

But they hadn't. That was the most

curious part of the whole incident. For a time, the car with the distinctive license plate lagged farther and farther behind, until there was not even a speck of red identifiable in the rear-view mirror.

And then, just outside Ventura, it suddenly reappeared.

A whisper of uneasiness tiptoed through Jenny's mind as she watched the car loom steadily closer. Was it only coincidence, she wondered, that brought them into contact with that same car again and again? She was reminded of a game of tag, where first one player and then another darts ahead. But sensible people didn't play games on a highway.

Her toe pressed harder on the accelerator. The old engine responded sluggishly to her demand for more speed, and after a few seconds Jenny was obliged to ease off again. It was futile to try to outdistance their pursuer, she thought resignedly. If, that is, he was really following them. Under the circumstances, it was hard to be sure. The driver of the small red automobile breezed smoothly past without even a glance in their direction.

Jenny rubbed her eyes. She was just tired, she decided — tired enough to let her imagination run off on all sorts of tangents. Undoubtedly she had crisscrossed positions with a score of cars that day. Paul's comment on the BYE plate was the only thing that had called that particular auto to her attention.

Dr. Avery must have noticed her gesture of fatigue. His voice broke into her mental debate.

"I hadn't realized it was so late," he apologized. "You must be exhausted, Jenny. I should have insisted on taking over the wheel long ago. In any case, I don't believe we should try to go much farther tonight."

"I agree, Clement." Miss Ursula had been studying the road map, and she mentioned that they would soon be passing through Santa Barbara. "Some hot food and a good night's sleep will refresh us all," she added. "Let's watch for a motel displaying a 'vacancy' sign."

Anxious as she was to reach the end of the journey, Jenny realized the wisdom of their decision. Obediently, she detoured off the main highway and guided the car through the city's beautiful residential district. A mile farther on, a winking neon sign drew their attention to an attractive inn. Before long, the party was comfortably settled in two large double rooms.

A hearty dinner and a steaming shower did much to revive Jenny's morale. She retired early to the cozy unit she shared with Miss Ursula. Snuggling down between the sheets of her twin bed, she sleepily remembered the maneuvers of the little red Volkswagen.

Had it really been following them? The notion seemed rather far-fetched now. But if so, she thought, they had neatly out-witted the other car. A smile curved about her lips as her eyelids fluttered shut. That sandy-haired driver would have a long wait if he had slowed down, expecting them to pass him again.

Sounds from the adjacent room woke her eight hours later. Jenny slipped out of bed and tiptoed to the window. It was a glorious morning, with the cloudless sky already tinted a deep azure blue. Best of all, a free-form swimming pool rippled invitingly only a few yards across the lawn.

Noiselessly, she opened her suitcase and pulled out the pretty print bathing suit that Mark had sent her last spring from Hono-lulu. She stepped into it, tucked her dark curls beneath a matching cap, then hurried outside and tapped at the next door.

"Paul," she called softly. "Are you

awake? How about an early-bird swim?"

Almost instantly he scampered out to join her.

Jenny smiled encouragingly as they poised together on the low diving board. "See — I told you we'd find lots to do!"

For nearly an hour they had the pool to themselves. When their fellow tourists began to appear, they toweled themselves to a tingling glow and padded back to their rooms.

Miss Ursula had the suitcases repacked and standing near the door when Jenny, clad in a sunny yellow slack suit, emerged from the bathroom.

"You look pretty as a spring bouquet, my dear," Miss Ursula complimented the girl. "How fortunate we are to have you with us."

"I'm the lucky one," Jenny answered, giving the older woman's hand an impulsive squeeze. "You don't know —"

A sharp rap at the door, followed by a call from the professor, interrupted her. Jenny had been feeling a trifle guilty about not telling the Averys the true reason for her desire to make the trip with them, but the appropriate moment to share the confidence had never seemed to arrive. Last night she had been too sleepy, and now —

"We're coming," she called back, stepping around the suitcases. This wasn't the time for a serious discussion, either. It would just have to wait.

Over breakfast they discussed the alternate roads north.

"Even though it's longer, we might make better time by taking the fast inland route," Jenny pointed out. "On the other hand, the old Coast Highway is supposed to be very scenic. It was originally traveled by the first Spanish settlers."

"Which would be the easiest for you?" Dr. Avery inquired.

Jenny confessed that in the past she had always traveled by train or airplane. "I don't imagine it would make much difference."

The professor winked at Miss Ursula. "Then, knowing my sister's love of scenery, and since Paul still hasn't seen his first whale, I suggest we take the coastal route."

Two hours later, Jenny had already begun to regret the decision. It wasn't that the map had been deceptive, exactly. Nothing could have been more scenic than the narrow two-lane road that snaked around camel's-hump curves and teetered on the brink of a breathtaking ocean view. Unfortunately, however, the frothing Pacific lay a hundred feet straight down, and jagged black rocks fringed the shoreline.

Nothing could have been lonelier, either. It was a desolate, uninhabited region, beautiful but untamed. The dazzling panorama didn't quite make up for the fact that if a motorist should encounter trouble, there was no one within fifty miles or more who could come to his assistance. Or her assistance, Jenny amended. She hoped fervently that the old black sedan was capable of withstanding this last rugged leg of their journey.

She tried to hide her concern from the others. "The view really is heavenly," she said. "I'm glad, though, that we filled up with gas before starting."

The professor, too, seemed aware of the potential danger.

"Keep as close to the mountainside as possible," he urged. "There is barely room for two cars to pass. If a truck were to come along —"

That didn't seen very likely, thought Jenny. The road might have been considered ideal by conquistadores on horseback, but modern truck drivers had more sense than to attempt to drive on a shoelace! It gave her a creepy feeling to realize that since leaving Morro Bay they had not seen another vehicle of any description.

The notion had scarcely formed in her mind when a brilliant flash of light was reflected in the rearview mirror. Jenny glanced up in surprise. She had been wrong — there was another car behind them.

At first only the glint of sunlight bouncing off its windshield was visible. Curves frequently hid the trailing car from sight. Eventually, though, the gap between the two automobiles lessened, and little by little she was able to distinguish the details of its appearance. It was red, she noted, and small. Bug sized, in fact — and bug-shaped.

Something close to panic welled in Jenny's throat. She choked it down, telling herself that it wasn't possible. This couldn't be the same car that had criss-crossed their path all day yesterday!

But that was a vain hope. The little Volkswagen drew to within a few car lengths of them, and the markings on its license plate became all too recognizable. B-Y-E . . .

Her gasp of recognition alarmed the professor. "Is something wrong?" he demanded. "Jenny, you're pale as a ghost!"

She nodded, tightening her grip on the

steering wheel as they rounded a corkscrew bend. "That car back there — it's been following us for the past two days!"

Dr. Avery swiveled quickly to stare at the pursuing auto. "I don't understand," he protested. "Why should anyone wish to trail us?"

Jenny swallowed hard, fighting back a sob. "I'm afraid it's my brother they're really after. You see, Mark disappeared —"

He listened without interruption while she blurted out the story told her by the two Shore Patrolmen.

"I knew there was something terribly wrong when I didn't hear from Mark in such a long time," she cried. "And then when the package arrived from San Francisco I decided to try to find him myself. Oh, I know I should have told you before! I meant to, honestly! But I didn't want to worry anyone else with my problems —"

"You must let us help you now," Miss Ursula spoke quietly from the back seat. Paul was cradled sleepily in her lap, but she leaned forward to pat Jenny's shoulder in reassurance. "What was in the package you received?"

Jenny drew a ragged breath and fished the tissue-wrapped image from her purse. She handed it to Dr. Avery.

"There was no message with the statuette. Only those three monkeys. It took me quite a long time to figure out what it meant, but now I'm sure it is Mark's way of telling me to trust him — to believe no evil of him."

Dr. Avery critically examined the little wood carving. His interest in art, and the many years he had spent in the Orient, qualified him to give an expert opinion.

"This is a fine piece of workmanship," he declared. "From the materials used, I would guess that it had been made in America. However, the craftsman who carved it was undoubtedly a Chinese." He glanced at Jenny. "Your interpretation of its meaning could be correct. But why do you believe your brother is in hiding?"

"It occurred to me that he could be involved in a secret government mission," she confessed. "I'm positive he isn't a deserter, or — or a traitor. But his disappearing like that scared me. I wanted to find him, to try to help." She raised her eyes to the rearview mirror. "That wasn't very sensible, was it? If that man back there is following me to Mark, I'll only get him into worse trouble!"

"We won't let that happen," Dr. Avery said staunchly. "Stay with us in Monterey.

In a few days we can drive up to San Francisco and try to locate the shop where the statuette was sold. The delay should lessen the chance of exposing your brother."

"I'm awfully grateful —"

A jarring thud chopped Jenny's sentence in half. The steering wheel spun dizzily beneath her hands. Its sudden whirling force jolted her sideways against the door. She hurled herself upright, instinctively lunging to recapture control of the wheel. There was no time to think or plan; she knew only that she must keep the clumsy old sedan from veering any further toward the opposite side of the road.

A lightning glance to the left confirmed her worst fears. There was no guard rail at this point, nothing to prevent them from plunging over the sheer face of the cliff onto those needle-sharp rocks below.

"Blowout!" she gasped, aiming her foot in swift short jabs at the brake pedal. "Hold on!"

Paul whimpered in terror as the car slewed wildly from side to side. Jenny held her breath, afraid to crash her full weight onto the brake. The loose gravel provided no traction for the straining tires, and a too sudden attempt to stop could overturn the car.

But a glimpse of the road ahead showed that she had no alternative. In a very few seconds they would reach the next curve. It looked sharp — too sharp, Jenny thought desperately. She had to halt the sedan's momentum somehow, or they would all go hurtling off into space!

Clenching her teeth on a silent prayer, she hammered the brake nearly to the floorboard. At the same time she wrenched the steering wheel with all her might, aiming the car straight in toward the sloping hillside. Brakes and tires shrieked in protest, their squeal mingling with the muffled groan that escaped from Dr. Avery's white lips.

Jenny was too busy to listen. At the last possible instant she swung the wheel out again. The dust-streaked fender grazed rock and clay, but she had calculated the distance correctly. The brakes shrilled a final time; the sedan lurched, straightened its course, and came to a trembling halt not five feet from the curve's inward bulge.

The thumping, careening ride had lasted no more than a minute, but to Jenny it had seemed like an hour-long nightmare.

"Oh, dear heaven!" she shivered. "What a scare! Is everyone all right?"

Three weak but thankful "yesses" were her response.

Jenny slumped against the seat cushions, still too shaken to think of anything but their narrow escape from death.

It wasn't until footsteps crunched up alongside and her door was jerked abruptly open that she remembered the little red Volkswagen.

She spun around in consternation. Two feet away stood the sandy-haired driver of the BYE car!

# Chapter Five

For a long half minute nobody said a word. Then the newcomer stooped and extended his hand to Jenny.

"Here, let me help you," he said in an unexpectedly gentle voice. "Think you can walk?"

"Yes, I — we're not injured," Jenny stammered.

She released his hand as soon as her feet touched the road, and turned back to assist Miss Ursula from the car. Paul hopped out also. His small round face was still pale, but he hurried to stand protectively in front of Jenny.

The stranger seemed bewildered by their defensive attitude. He was even more astonished when Dr. Avery rounded the far side of the sedan and confronted him with a blunt question.

"See here," the professor snapped. "Have you been following us?"

The young man backed up a step. Behind the horn-rimmed glasses his steady gray eyes took on a puzzled expression, but this quickly faded.

"To be perfectly frank, I have," he admitted. His pleasant face was brightened by the beginnings of a grin. "I can explain, though. My car has been having fuel-line problems — it gave me trouble all day yesterday. It would go along fine for an hour or two, then I'd have to slow practically to a crawl to get it unplugged."

Jenny and Paul exchanged relieved glances. So this was the explanation for the Volkswagen's speed-up and lag-behind tactics!

"I stopped overnight in Gaviota and had a mechanic take a look at the darn thing," the young man continued. "It seems to be running all right now. I couldn't afford any more delays, however, so I decided to take the shortest route to Monterey. At least it looked shorter on the map!"

He gestured expressively at their wilderness surroundings. "Anyway, when I spotted your car ahead of me, I tried to keep close behind in case something went wrong and I needed help."

"Please accept our apologies," the professor said in some embarrassment. "As it turns out, we are the ones who require assistance. I am Clement Avery. May I present my sister, Ursula, my grandson,

Paul, and our friend, Miss Jenny Sheldon."

"My name is Russell MacAllister." He gripped the professor's hand. "Are you by any chance the Dr. Avery who is to teach a course in languages at the Center for International Understanding and Cooperation? If so, I believe you will be my instructor."

Fully reassured now, Dr. Avery acknowledged that the Monterey Center was their destination. Miss Ursula murmured a word or two to help smoothe over the awkward situation, then she and Paul strolled across the road to gaze down at the surf pounding against the rocks far below.

"That misunderstanding was entirely my fault," Jenny said contritely. "We kept seeing your car, and — I'm terribly sorry."

"You're forgiven — this time," Russell MacAllister laughed. "My behavior did look rather suspicious, I suppose, although it never occurred to me that anyone would mistake me for a highway bandit."

His friendliness quickly put Jenny at ease. "Dr. Avery spoke very highly of the Center's work," she remarked. "Are you one of the volunteers who will be going abroad?"

"Yes, to India," he nodded. "And speaking of going, I think we had better see about getting this procession under way again. You *are* equipped with a spare tire, I hope?"

"I hope so, too!" Jenny gazed apprehensively at the bleak cliffs that hemmed them off from civilization. "This isn't exactly my idea of a resort area. Thank goodness we didn't attempt to drive through it at night!"

Moving back toward the sedan, they found Dr. Avery wrestling with the catch on the luggage compartment.

"Let me do that for you, sir," Russ offered.

He wasted no time in unloading the spare tire and jack. Within a few minutes he had the car propped up and was energetically prying off the ruined rubber tube.

Jenny was impressed by the efficient way in which he tackled the greasy job. Not too many motorists, she thought, would have taken the time and trouble to assist a carload of total strangers. Her curiosity about the slender young man increased as she watched him bend his back to the task.

He's certainly an unusual sort of person, she mused. I wonder what made him decide to go to India, of all places?

It was such a strange country, half a world away —

"That ought to do it," Russ announced, twirling the last bolt into place. He hopped up and carefully manipulated the jack until the car was once again resting on all four wheels.

Paul and Miss Ursula had returned to watch the last part of the operation. "It looks good as new," the little boy said admiringly. "I was scared when we had the blowout. What made the tire pop?"

Russ bent over and retrieved a glittering object that had lodged in the tube. "Here's the culprit," he said, holding out a small, sharp piece of glass. "Some litterbug probably tossed it out his window, not realizing the damage things like this can do. Incidentally," he added to Jenny, "that was a very skillful bit of driving. I don't see how you kept the car from going over."

"Neither do I, now that I think of it," she admitted. "Fortunately, I didn't have time to do much thinking then."

Dr. Avery gave her a fatherly pat on the shoulder. "People show their true character in times of crisis, Jenny. You coped with that emergency far better than most older persons could have."

Turning back to Russ, he thanked the

young man for his assistance. "That job would have taken me hours. We are most grateful for your help."

"Glad to have been of service," Russell MacAllister replied. His eyes met Jenny's with a teasing twinkle. "I'll follow you the rest of the way in to Monterey, if that's all right."

She burst out laughing, thinking how silly her unfounded fears had proved to be. "We absolutely insist that you do so!"

The last fifty miles of their trip passed quickly. Late in the afternoon they rolled into the picturesque seacoast town. After stopping for directions, Jenny guided the car past a number of wharves and fishing piers until, at the very edge of the harbor, they found the address they had been seeking.

She stared with interest at the low rectangular building. Its uncluttered exterior sparkled with a fresh coat of white paint, but there was nothing about it that even remotely resembled a school.

Miss Ursula echoed her thoughts. "What an unusual location! Right on the waterfront," she observed. "It looks like some sort of warehouse."

Dr. Avery chuckled. "That was the purpose for which the building was originally used. Up until a year or two ago, this was a loading and storage station for the Marsh Shipping Line. Hammond Marsh donated the facilities to the Center when he retired from business." He flung open the car door. "Warehouse or not, I'm sure we will find it adequately equipped."

Just then, the now-familiar little red auto pulled in to the curb beside the sedan. Russ MacAllister jumped out to join them as they started up the neat cement walk that led to the front entrance. His sandy hair looked freshly combed, and Jenny noticed that he had changed into a clean sport shirt.

There was an eager expression on his boyish face. "The end of one journey, and the start of another," he murmured, almost to himself.

Dr. Avery led the party inside. They found themselves in a large sunlit room, which bustled with activity. Groups of people were scattered informally around various tables. Some of them were reading or studying, while others appeared to be involved in a lively discussion.

Near the door stood a reception desk. A girl only slightly older than Jenny stood up and hurried forward to greet them.

"We are so happy you're here." She

smiled when the professor had identified himself. "Please be seated while I call Dr. Wynne. He has been anxiously awaiting your arrival."

Jenny looked curiously around during their short wait. Doors opened onto the reception room from both sides of the building, and as people entered and left she caught brief intriguing glimpses of laboratories and classrooms.

"Isn't this exciting?" she whispered to Russ. "It all looks so friendly, yet well organized, too. Will you be spending much time here before your departure?"

"A couple of months, I imagine," he answered. "It all depends on when the next ship is scheduled to leave."

Jenny found his reply somewhat puzzling. Ships sailed from California to the Far East with great frequency, she knew. Wouldn't the volunteers' reservations have been made long ago? There was no chance to ask anything further, though, since at that moment a tall, hearty-looking man with iron-gray hair and a genial expression emerged from a side door and advanced toward them.

"We are honored to have you with us, Dr. Avery," he said, clasping the older man's hand. "I am Derek Wynne. I direct the

Center's operations and try to coordinate all our efforts." He bestowed a smile on Miss Ursula and Jenny. His cordiality increased still more when Russ was introduced.

"Welcome to the Center, Mr. Mac-Allister," he said. "Your work has promoted a great deal of interest here. I'm looking forward to discussing the process at some length. First, though, let me show you through the building."

Jenny held back until the director's gesture made it clear that the entire party was included in the invitation. Then taking Paul's hand, she glanced anxiously at Miss Ursula.

"I hope this won't be too tiring for you."

"I wouldn't dream of missing this chance to tour the Center," Miss Ursula declared. "Clement has talked of nothing else for months."

Although Jenny was much less familiar with the project than any of the others, she felt her enthusiasm grow as they proceeded through classrooms furnished in an almost spartan fashion, peeked into conference rooms, and continued on past two laboratory workshops. Derek Wynne then ushered the group into an as yet unfinished section of the former warehouse.

"We'll be setting up a clinic here within

the next few months," he explained. "All the facilities you have seen thus far have been for the training of our own volunteers. We have kept the cost of equipment down to a bare minimum so that the major portion of our funds can be dedicated to the work we hope to accomplish abroad."

"How will a clinic fit in with your program?" Russ wanted to know.

Dr. Wynne gazed proudly around the roughed-in space. "It will provide training for young interns and student nurses from all over Asia," he said. "The techniques they learn here can be put to excellent use once they return to their own countries."

"This is all that I expected, and more," Dr. Avery declared. "I am delighted to have a share in such a worthwhile project."

"Good. Time, as you know, is a crucial matter. If you wish, you can begin your course of instruction tomorrow."

Dr. Wynne smiled, taking Miss Ursula's arm as he started back toward the reception room. Paul trotted along beside his grandfather, and Jenny followed with Russ.

"This is a fascinating place," she said. "I've been wondering what your part in it is. Are you a doctor?"

"Nope. I water things." He grinned mysteriously. "If you're really interested, I could tell you more about it this evening. Dr. Wynne mentioned that he is holding an open house tonight for the staff and their families, as well as for the new volunteers. You will come, won't you?"

"It depends on the Averys." Jenny hesitated. "I am not part of their family, you know. I'm only staying with them for a short time to help out. But the open house sounds interesting, and —"

"And you'd like to know what sort of things I water." Russ laughed. "Do come. Tomorrow I start the battle of the textbooks. I may spin out the tale as Scheherazade did, to persuade you to help me with my homework."

"What a threat!"

Jenny could make no definite promise, however. She quickened her footsteps to catch up with the others. At the front entrance she found Derek Wynne preparing to escort the Averys to the house where they would be staying for the summer. There was time for only a wave to Russ, then she was climbing into the black sedan again.

The route Dr. Wynne chose led them out of the downtown area and through several lovely residential areas fronting the sea. Before long, both cars were toiling up a steep hill. Near the top the Center's director turned into a secluded driveway. Jenny applied her brakes, awed by the beauty of the Spanish-style house that confronted them. Odd-shaped Moorish windows peeked out from the dazzlingly white adobe walls; grilled balconies and a red tile roof added a graceful charm to the scene.

"I'm sure you will be comfortable here," Dr. Wynne said, ushering them inside. "There is a small private beach at the foot of your rear garden, and it has the advantage of being near Mr. Marsh's home. He lives at the crest of the hill, about a quarter of a mile away."

"We must thank him for his generosity as soon as possible," Miss Ursula said when the bedrooms, baths, and other appointments of the home had been pointed out to her.

"He may be present at the open house tonight," Dr. Wynne replied. "Mr. Marsh is quite elderly and in poor health nowadays, but he is genuinely interested in everyone connected with our project. I know he is looking forward to renewing your old friendship, Dr. Avery."

"In that case, we shall be happy to attend," the professor promised.

The house was beautifully decorated,

and furnished in an authentic Spanish style. Jenny would have liked to spend more time admiring the handsomely carved pieces, but there were more important things to be done just then. Signs of exhaustion were plainly visible on Miss Ursula's face, and Dr. Avery's shoulders drooped with fatigue. She persuaded them both to sit down; then she and Paul hurried out to the kitchen. To her delight, she found the cupboards well stocked with food, and an array of fresh dairy products in the refrigerator.

"Goodness! Mr. Marsh is certainly a thoughtful host," she murmured.

Paul set out milk and eggs and butter while she opened some canned soup. "Grandpa says he's a rich millionaire," the little boy piped.

"I guess he must be." Jenny laughed as she scrambled eggs and grated cheese for an omelet. "It's nice that he is putting his money to good use, helping people in other countries who are less fortunate than we."

She popped bread into the toaster, set out place mats and dishes, and within a few minutes had a tasty meal ready.

"That was delicious, Jenny," Miss Ursula complimented her half an hour later. "This was exactly what we needed. Even so, I don't believe I feel up to attending a party tonight, and I suspect that Paul won't be able to keep his eyes open much longer. Are you too tired to drive Clement over to Dr. Wynne's house? He would have difficulty in locating it by himself."

"I'll be glad to," Jenny agreed.

By seven-thirty, the suitcases were unpacked, the dishes washed and stacked away, and Paul was already tucked into bed. A brisk shower helped evaporate Jenny's weariness. The bathroom's moist atmosphere had also steamed the wrinkles out of her becoming green knit dress, and as she zipped it up the back she found herself looking forward to her next encounter with Russ MacAllister.

"I'm as bad as Pandora," she giggled, giving her short black tresses a final pat. "But I must admit I'm curious. What on earth kind of job is 'watering things'?"

Not long afterward, Jenny realized that it wasn't only his mysterious occupation that intrigued her. They had scarcely been ushered into Dr. Wynne's home when Russ, who had been in the middle of a laughing group of young people, spied them and came hurrying over. With his horn-rimmed glasses, and wearing a neat blue suit and tie, he looked almost scholarly, but the humorous twinkle in his gray eyes ruined the sober effect.

"Hello," he said after greeting Dr. Avery. "I see you couldn't resist the bait. Come along and I'll introduce you to some of my new friends."

Jenny smiled her acceptance. In the past few days she had wondered now and then about the sort of persons who would willingly sacrifice two years of their lives for an ideal. She had come to the conclusion that they must be extraordinary individuals. But as Russ drew her into the knot of chattering young adults she could see no outward difference between them and her own college acquaintances.

They all seemed intent on listening to a redheaded youth who looked as if he would be more at home on a football field than in a jungle clinic.

". . . ship should be ready to leave by mid-August," he was saying. "This time, though, I doubt that they'll reveal the sailing date ahead of time. No sense giving the pirates an even greater advantage —"

Nate Benedict broke off at the sound of Jenny's muffled gasp.

"Hi!" he grinned, jumping up to offer her a chair. "You must be the damsel-in-distress of Highway One that Russ mentioned."

"Yes," she nodded. "And I do apologize for interrupting. But did you say *pirates?*"

# Chapter Six

"That's what I said," the redheaded boy repeated.

"Twentieth-century-style pirates. They've abandoned their peg legs and eye patches, but according to all accounts they still fly the traditional skull and crossbones."

Jenny sank into the chair that Nate had vacated. "In this day and age — it's unbelievable!"

"Maybe so, but that doesn't make it any less true," Nate assured her.

A wide-eyed couple in their early twenties introduced themselves as Deedee and Bruce Jay. They obligingly scooted down on the couch so that Russ could sit near Jenny.

"I don't blame you for being shocked," Russ said. "I've just been finding out about it myself. Weird as it sounds, two of the Center's own ships have been attacked on the high seas. The pirates hijacked the entire cargoes of both vessels; tons of medical supplies, food, seeds, and farm machinery were stolen."

Jenny's thoughts raced backward to a time, six or seven days earlier, when Debra Tucker had made some excited comment about pirates. The Shore Patrolmen's visit and her desperate worry about Mark had driven the incident from her mind, but now she remembered her friend's misgivings.

"Have any of the ocean liners been bothered?" she asked.

"No." The answer came from a pretty blonde girl whose name, Jenny learned later, was Elaine Kendall. "The Marsh Shipping Line furnishes ships and crews for the Center's use. They're fairly old, slow-moving vessels — just right for our purposes but completely helpless against the hijackers' speedy cutter."

"Why, that's terrible!" Jenny exclaimed, her indignation flaring. "Can't the Coast Guard do something?"

Nate Benedict nodded soberly. "The last ship the Center dispatched made it through okay, thanks to a naval escort. There were rumors that the Government stepped in when word filtered through that our goods were showing up on the black market. But the Navy is needed in plenty of other places right now. They can't keep on riding shotgun for us."

What a bitter disappointment for everyone connected with the project, Jenny thought, to learn that their precious supplies and equipment had fallen into the hands of sea going thugs.

Pony-tailed Deedee Jay echoed this pensive reflection aloud.

"Think of all the pokey old tankers and tramp steamers that are constantly crossing the Pacific," she remarked. "None of them have been molested. It looks as if the hijackers are concentrating exclusively on the Center's ships." Apprehension tinged her earnest blue eyes. "Do you suppose terrorists could be using this method to scare our people out of Asia?"

"Why us?" Nate asked reasonably. "We're trying to help others, not take over their countries."

"If a subversive group is behind these raids, they have a well-trained lookout stationed right here on the Peninsula!" Elaine Kendall declared. "That second ship sailed from Monterey without one word of advance publicity. Yet it hadn't got ten miles out to sea before it was looted by the pirates!"

Jenny shivered. It was frightening to think that the ominous slogan, "Big Brother Is Watching," might apply right here in their own country.

Russ noticed her distress. "Let's all stay on the lookout for any unauthorized stranger hanging around the Center," he suggested quietly. "Meanwhile, the less said about our suspicions, the better. The authorities are bound to be working on the 'spy' angle too, and we don't want to alarm their quarry prematurely."

"A lot of loose talk might also scare off any new recruits who might be thinking of joining the program," Bruce Jay added. "Besides, we're missing a good party by all this serious discussion. Isn't that Hammond Marsh who just came in?"

Along with the others, Jenny glanced toward the doorway. Her eyes rested for a moment on an elderly man in a wheelchair. He was almost broomstick thin, but his alert eyes showed a keen sparkle. She watched as he greeted a dozen people in quick succession.

"Dr. Avery and Mr. Marsh became friends when they were both living in the Orient many years ago," she mentioned to Russ. "I hope they have a chance to enjoy their reunion. Mr. Marsh certainly seems to be popular."

"With good reason," Russ agreed. "Hammond Marsh's millions gave the Center its start. In addition to that, he takes a real interest in the people working under his sponsorship. I wonder who the fellow with him is."

The tall, darkly good-looking young man who had accompanied Hammond Marsh into the room had not escaped Jenny's observant eye. He moved along behind the wheelchair with the easy self-assurance of an invited guest. But although he was greeted cordially by Dr. Wynne and his staff, Jenny had a hunch that this second newcomer was not one of the Center "team." His deep tan and long, swinging stride suggested an outdoor occupation.

She held her gaze an instant too long. The handsome stranger looked up, and across the room his eyes met hers.

Embarrassment at having been caught staring reddened Jenny's cheeks. Quickly she turned back to Russ.

"What a lot of people there are here! It would help if everyone wore name tags, like delegates at a convention."

"Or children on their first day at kindergarten. But I imagine that inside of a week we'll all have each other sorted out," Russ replied optimistically. He gestured toward the buffet table, which was laden with an array of delectable food. "Would you like something to eat?"

The room had grown very crowded by the time they reached the end of the serving line. Carefully balancing cups and plates, they made their way outside to a wide balcony jutting out over the sea. Jenny set her plate on the concrete safety ledge and peered down a little breathlessly at the surf, which swirled and bubbled a few yards beneath the cantilevered overhang.

"Even at night they have a glorious view from here," Russ remarked, bringing up a couple of deck hairs.

The evening sky was clear and starry. Gazing out over the placid ocean, Jenny wondered how far a ship could be seen from a vantage point such as this before it dipped beyond the horizon.

"Do you suppose Elaine is right?" she asked. "About the pirates having a lookout here on the coast, I mean? It seems so incredible that violence of that nature can ever shatter this peaceful scene."

"The idea sounds logical," Russ admitted. "Nate was telling me that Elaine's husband was aboard that second ship when it was raided. Walt Kendall is a doctor, and Elaine is finishing up her M.D. training next month. They had planned to sail together, but Walt went on ahead when that tsunami hit New Guinea."

"Think of all the medicine that must have gone out on that ship with him. How disgusting to think of all that life-giving serum going to waste!"

Jenny furrowed her brow, reflecting, on second thought, that the serum had probably been put to good use elsewhere. The pirates' looting tactics sounded more like robbery for gain than like an enemy-inspired plot. At least no one had been injured by the buccaneers — yet.

"Let's hope those sea-going highwaymen are captured before your group sails," she added. "By the way, you promised to tell me about your own work."

Russ smiled. "It's a pretty dull story. Actually, I was just casting around for an excuse to see you again."

"You and Scheherazade!"

"Nothing so romantic as the *Arabian Nights*, I'm afraid."

His grin disappeared. "For a long time scientists have been hoping to find a simple and inexpensive way to use sea water for irrigation. The problem interested me, too, since my Dad is a rancher and we sometimes lost our crops during a dry spell. While I was in college I had a lucky break and hit on a method that didn't involve using tons of expensive machinery. It worked when we tried it out at home. Since then, several other communities have put the process into operation."

"How exciting! Are you going to experiment with your idea in India?"

He nodded. "They've had a two-year famine over there, and the drought situation is growing increasingly critical. The United States, as well as other countries, is doing their best to feed those people, but that is only a temporary solution. I think I can help them grow their own crops." Russ set his empty plate on the ledge. "So — here I am. On my way, if I can manage to learn enough Hindi to see me through."

"You will," Jenny predicted confidently. "Dr. Avery is a wonderful teacher. Besides, this sounds important enough to outweigh any language consideration. Your project could save thousands of people from starvation!"

Before Russ could answer, the terrace door opened and a half-dozen young people emerged onto the balcony. In the strong moonlight Jenny recognized Nate Benedict and Elaine Kendall, as well as a trio of medical technicians to whom she had been introduced earlier.

Elaine smiled gaily at Jenny and Russ.

"Hi, you two! It's heavenly out here, especially after all the noise and smoke inside. Have you met Van Gilbert yet?"

She looked over her shoulder at the sixth newcomer, drawing him into the circle of conversation. Extending her hand politely, Jenny found herself staring into a pair of dark brown eyes that twinkled with amusement.

"Hello again," said the young man who had hovered so attentively behind Hammond Marsh's wheelchair. "If my uncle didn't need me at home, I'd be highly tempted to sign up for an Asian tour myself. All the best-looking girls in the state seem to be going."

For the second time that evening Jenny felt a blush tingle against her skin. She hoped the light was dim enough to keep anyone else from noticing.

"I wish I were talented enough to be one of the Center's volunteers," she said. "To tell the truth, though, I'm only here as Dr. Avery's chauffeur. May I present my friend, Russell MacAllister?"

Russ had been looking a trifle annoyed at the intrusion, but he accepted Van Gilbert's hand courteously.

"Pleased to meet you," he said. "Mr. Marsh is your uncle? We're all very grateful to him for the fine work he is sponsoring."

Elaine had seated herself in one of the deck chairs. She leaned back, filling her lungs with the fresh air, and gestured at the starlit sky.

"Not a hint of fog tonight! Why don't you conjure up more evenings like this for us, Van?"

"Don't think I wouldn't like to. But old Mother Nature doesn't always oblige." Seeing that Russ and Jenny were puzzled by this reference to the elements, he explained. "I'm a meteorologist — weather man, so-called. One of those much maligned second-guessers who are right only seventy-eight percent of the time."

"That sounds like a pretty good average to me," Russ chuckled. Then he glanced at his wristwatch. "Time I went and thanked my host and hostess. Have you any idea how long Dr. Avery planned to stay, Jenny?"

"No, although I doubt that it will be very much longer." Gathering up their dishes, she smiled good night at the group. "I've enjoyed meeting you. Bye!"

Stepping back into the living room, they noticed that the crowd was beginning to thin out. Jenny looked around for Dr.

Avery and spied him just rising from a corner seat next to Hammond Marsh's wheelchair.

"Perfect timing!" she dimpled. "Good luck with your studies, Russ. Perhaps we'll run into each other again before you leave."

Behind the horn-rimmed glasses his gray eyes held a smiling promise. "No 'perhaps' about it! Just give me a few days to get organized, and I'll be pounding on your door. After all, my ship doesn't sail until sometime in August."

Jenny made no mention of the fact that she would probably have left Monterey long before then. She didn't really belong here, she recalled wistfully. As soon as she found Mark —

Dr. Avery's arrival at her side forced these thoughts to the back of her mind. Anxiously aware of the lines of fatigue that etched his face, she grasped his arm and assisted him down the stairs to the car.

"You look terribly tired," she sympathized. "But I'm glad you were able to manage a private chat with Mr. Marsh. Did you enjoy the reunion?"

He nodded soberly. "It was good to visit with my old friend again. But after what I had seen today, the news he gave me was disturbing." A deep sigh escaped his lips. "Hammond is gravely distressed by the attacks on his ships. If it happens again — if another cargo is hijacked — he intends to withdraw his support from the Center!"

# Chapter Seven

The morning following Dr. Wynne's party, Jenny awoke to dazzling sunlight flooding her room. She bounced upright in the bed, blinking at the unfamiliar surroundings.

"Heavens!" she giggled, throwing on her robe. "I must have been tired last night. Imagine falling asleep without even closing the drapes!"

A sliding glass door framed a tiny balcony just outside her window. Jenny tugged it open and stepped out. Leaning over an ornamental but sturdy wrought-iron railing, she peered down into a well-tended flower garden. A little gated fence at the rear of the yard led onto a golden crescent of beach. The sand above the outgoing tide looked as if it had been freshly laundered and spread out to dry.

"Oh, glory, what a day!" she exulted, skipping back inside to change into Bermuda shorts and a sleeveless blouse. She hurried downstairs as soon as her room was tidy. An appetizing aroma of baking pancakes and sizzling bacon wafted from the kitchen.

"Good morning, Jenny," Miss Ursula greeted her. "Sit down, dear. I started this batch when I heard you moving around upstairs. Clement left for the Center a short time ago, and Paul has been up for hours, just dying to start exploring the beach. He wants you to go with him."

"Nothing would suit me better," Jenny admitted, reaching for the syrup. "After glimpsing that view from my window, I can understand why people become beach-combers!"

A few minutes later she and Paul were hunting through the warm, dry sand in search of shells. The tide was almost completely out now, and by the time they reached the boulder-strewn point that formed the right-hand boundary of their property, the little boy had his pail half full of delicately tinted specimens.

"End of the line, pardner. At least on this side," said Jenny, starting to turn back.

"The other end is blocked off, too," Paul informed her, pointing. "See that fence? It goes all the way down into the water."

"How peculiar!" Jenny shaded her eyes and saw that he was correct. A sagging wooden barrier extended from the edge of the steeply sloping hillside, crossed the sand, and dipped beyond the low-tide point into the surf. As they approached the fence she made out the lettering on a large sign dangling from the weathered rails: "NO TRESPASSING!"

"My, those people really do value their privacy," she observed.

There was nothing to prevent them from walking as far as the fence, however. As they neared the warning poster Jenny saw that the Averys' house was not nearly so isolated as she had thought. Another home teetered on the hillside only a short distance up the slope, but the sheer rise of the cliff between the two dwellings separated them more effectively than acres of flatland could have.

Gazing upward, Jenny felt a prickle of apprehension. Although no one was in sight, she had the uncomfortable feeling that hostile eyes were watching her every move.

"Let's go back, Jenny. I don't like it here." Paul tugged urgently at her arm. His small bare feet made hurried tracks across the sand until they had carried him a safe distance from the fence.

Jenny followed more slowly. Once or twice she glanced back over her shoulder, wondering whether there was any concrete basis for the trepidation that almost-broodingly silent house had aroused in her. Still nothing stirred, but she was sure that the uneasy sensation had not been entirely caused by her imagination. Paul had felt it, too.

She caught up with him when the angle of the hill had once more cut the neighboring house off from view. "Did something happen over there that scared you?" she asked curiously.

"No, it was just sort of creepy," Paul answered. "He had a spyglass, and I could tell he was looking straight at us."

Jenny's mouth fell open in astonishment. "Who?"

"The man in the window, of course. You're taller than me, so maybe the sun coming over the hill got in your eyes," he declared. "But I saw him — plain as anything. The look on his face said 'go away!' "

"Then that's just what we'll do. Go away and stay away. You see, honey, some people have reasons for not wanting to be neighborly."

Jenny couldn't think of any reasons offhand, but the little boy accepted her explanation without question. He was gazing discontentedly at his pailful of shells.

"Most of these are chipped around the edges," he complained. "I'll bet we could find some better ones farther out in the water."

"Probably." Jenny agreed that the tumbling action of the waves gave the shells quite a battering. Even so, she hesitated to allow Paul to venture very far beyond the shoreline.

"I don't suppose it would hurt to wade out just a little way," she conceded. "I'll go first to make sure you don't walk into a hole."

"Aw, gee, Jenny! I'm an awfully good swimmer." Ignoring the protest, she kicked off her sandals and took a few steps into the frothing surf.

"Brrr!" She shivered. "I think a glacier must have melted out here!"

After the first frigid impact, they gradually became accustomed to the water's iciness. Only a few tangles of seaweed cluttered the ocean floor, and peering down through the bubbles, they located three or four undamaged shells. Paul tucked them carefully into his pocket. When the water reached his waistline, Jenny motioned for him to stop.

"That's far enough, my goose-pimply friend. All ashore!"

Paul grimaced in disgust. "There must be a trillion jillion shells still out here!"

"What would you do with so many?" Jenny laughed, and steered him toward the beach. "We'll come out again soon, when the water is warmer."

"Well — okay." Cheered by her promise, Paul walked obediently ahead. Jenny sloshed along behind him, trying to keep her teeth from chattering.

Suddenly a flash of light from the hillside dazzled her eyes. She jerked her head up, focusing on the spot from which the glare had come. From this distance out, she had a perfect view of the mysteriously fenced house — and of the man behind the spyglass.

Paul had been right about that, Jenny thought. And he hadn't misread the watcher's expression, either.

Most emphatically it said "Go Away!"

It was late afternoon when Dr. Avery returned home from his first teaching session at the Center. He looked pleased with the day's progress, but tired, too. Seeing this, Jenny decided against mentioning their peculiar neighbor to him just then.

After all, it isn't against the law to be unfriendly, she reasoned with herself, relieving the professor of an armload of books. That man didn't threaten us, or anything. He was just — watching.

She frowned uneasily, puzzled by the unwavering vigilance she had glimpsed in the face half hidden behind the spyglass. The man's expression had been one of grim alertness. Was he looking for something in particular, she wondered, or did he merely stand there, hour after hour, focusing his lens on everyone and everything that came into sight?

The riddle seemed to have no answer. Jenny shrugged, and carried the books into the study. She glanced with interest at the volumes as she placed them on the desk. The stack included basic language primers as well as histories of several Asian nations.

"It looks to me as if you intend to do more homework than your students," she chided Dr. Avery. "Don't forget, this is supposed to be your vacation."

He smiled at her concern. "I am due for a sabbatical leave next year. I will have twelve months to rest then, if I wish. Right now there is much to be done, and so little time in which to accomplish it. They have a great deal to learn, these young people — a whole new language, a civilization completely unlike ours —"

With a sigh, he turned away from the desk. "Besides, this may be the last group of volunteers to travel to Asia under the Center's auspices. I want to do the best I can for them."

"Was Mr. Marsh really serious about withdrawing his support?" Jenny asked in distress. "Dr. Wynne had such high hopes for the new clinic." She thought of Russ, Elaine, Nate, and the others, who were approaching the task of aiding the less fortunate peoples of the world with such eagerness. "It would be a shame to have the work stop now!"

"I agree. But, interested as he is in the Center, Hammond looks upon this piracy as a personal insult. He built the Marsh fleet almost single-handedly, and even though he has retired from actively running the company, he feels that this menace may jeopardize the Line's prestige," Clement Avery explained. "I believe he regards those ships as a substitute for a family of his own."

"I met his nephew last night," Jenny remarked. "Van Gilbert certainly seems devoted to Mr. Marsh."

The professor nodded. "That is so. Hammond told me that the boy is his only living relative. Still, a nephew can hardly take the place of a wife and children, or grandchildren. And speaking of my grandson —"

"Paul is out in the kitchen polishing his shells," Jenny laughed. "We collected a few of them from the ocean bed, and I'm sure he would be still swimming toward Hawaii if I hadn't insisted that he return to shore."

Dr. Avery beamed his approval. "I'm glad you are here to help look after him, Jenny. It would please us all very much if you would consent to spend the rest of the summer with us."

"You and Miss Ursula have both been very kind to me," Jenny said sincerely. "And I love Paul. He's as dear to me as if he were my own little brother. But I'm frantically worried about Mark. I must try to find him!"

"In that case, we will drive up to San Francisco on Saturday," Dr. Avery promised. "Perhaps your little statuette will bring us good luck."

Jenny had no choice but to postpone her quest until then. Saturday was still two days off, however, and each morning she anxiously scanned the newspapers in hope of finding some mention of the missing naval officer. Her search proved futile. Setting aside the front section of the *Chronicle* on Friday morning, she consoled herself by remembering the strange gift Mark had sent her. It proved at least that no terrible accident had befallen him. He must still be alive!

As she cleared away the breakfast dishes she told herself that San Francisco wasn't really such a big city. And it wasn't as if they had no starting place for their search. The three monkeys were a valuable clue.

Jenny wasn't accustomed to having so much leisure time. Always before, there had been classes for which to study, her work at the library to keep her occupied, and plenty of friends with whom to plan some activity or other. But here in Monterey she knew practically no one, and even caring for Paul didn't begin to occupy all her time. To combat boredom, she hauled out the vacuum cleaner and gave the upstairs of the house a thorough dusting. This finished, and with half an hour yet to go until lunch time, she strolled outside.

Until the door closed behind her, Jenny had had no particular destination in mind. Then as she turned onto the sidewalk she caught a glimpse of a secluded house, its roof barely visible above a thick hedge of cypress that rimmed the borders of the next yard up the hill.

Her previous curiosity returned. With luck, she thought, she might encounter their glowering neighbor. It would be fun to find out about him — to see whether he was actually as cross and antisocial as he had appeared. Perhaps she and Paul had been mistaken about the man behind the spyglass. He could be an avid gardener, who had built the fence to protect his property from careless picknickers. Or —

But that was the only plausible excuse she could conjure up, and even that sounded pretty flimsy. Flowers didn't grow in sand!

Continuing along the steep incline, Jenny heard the putt-putt-putt of a toiling engine. A tiny vehicle, painted red, white, and blue, and with the words "U.S. Mail" stenciled on its cab, labored up alongside her. It drew ahead and hiccuped to the curb about half a block away. A postman hopped out and strode across the sidewalk. In a minute he was on his way again.

Jenny walked faster. So quick a delivery must mean that the mailbox stood well out in front of the house, like those in rural areas. There might be a name on the box —

There was. "A. Briswald," Jenny read,

squinting at the bold fresh lettering as she approached.

So intent was she on identifying the name that she didn't see the woman crossing the lawn until they had nearly collided.

"Oh!" Jenny pulled back a step and beamed her friendliest smile at the woman. Although she was not really old, she looked faded, bleached out almost, like something left too long in the sun. It was the lack of any color at all that gave the impression of a withered plant. Her hair was neither light nor dark, but a lifeless gray, and the apron covering her tall, gaunt frame was of the same dull shade.

"Hello. I'm staying with the Averys, who just moved in next door," Jenny said. "We were hoping to meet some of our neighbors soon. Are you Mrs. Briswald?"

The woman nodded hastily. "Yes. Yes, I am." Her hand darted jerkily into the mailbox and pulled out a couple of advertising circulars. "It's a nice place to live," she conceded.

"Simply beautiful!" Jenny agreed. "That ocean view —"

She never had a chance to finish the sentence. From the house came an irate bellow.

"Martha! Martha, come in here!"

The woman's pale eyes widened in alarm. Her "good-bye" was hurled over her shoulder as she scuttled up the curving flagstone walk.

Jenny had never been so dumbfounded in her entire life. For a full minute she stared open-mouthed at the hurrying figure. Then starting to turn away, she caught sight of a white rectangle lying on the grass.

"Oh, wait!" she called, picking up the envelope that Mrs. Briswald had dropped.

But the front door had already banged shut. There was no response from the shuttered windows.

Slowly Jenny straightened up. She had no choice but to replace the letter in the mailbox. She opened the metal hinge and started to drop it in. As she did so, her eyes fell on the scrawled address.

"Captain Amos Bohling, 1341 —"

Bohling! Jenny frowned. She closed the mailbox and sent a last speculative look at the silent house. *But their name is Briswald. Or is it?*

# Chapter Eight

As Jenny had reminded herself the day before, San Francisco wasn't really such a large city. In size and population it couldn't begin to compare with New York, Los Angeles, or Chicago. Nevertheless, her spirits nosedived as she eyed the crowds thronging Market Street, and sank even lower when she turned the car up bustling Grant Avenue.

How was she ever going to locate Mark among all these people?

But it was impossible to stay disheartened for long. In the year since her last visit she had almost forgotten how lovely the city was. Lovely — and unique. Flower vendors hawked their wares in front of smart glass-fronted shops; tiny hideaway restaurants nestled alongside glamorous hotels; sleek limousines and rickety jalopies alike inched their way around the clattering, clanging cable cars. And above it all, almost like twin crowns in the city's hair, hung the majestic bridges.

"Look Oh, Jenny, look!" Paul could

hardly sit still. "Did you ever see such a funny building?"

"It's a pagoda," she told him. "A mile or two farther on you'll see places that look exactly like parts of Italy. And in the Mission District many people cling to the ways of Old Mexico. That's all part of the fun of visiting here."

They had definitely entered the Chinese sector now. Lofty buildings gave way to cramped, dingy little shops huddled together along narrow streets that seemed more like alleys. The signs were painted in picturesque Oriental characters.

Jenny glanced uncertainly at Dr. Avery.

"This is a good place to begin looking," he decided. "It is possible the statuette came from one of the big import stores, but somehow I doubt it. It looks like the work of some meticulous craftsman who is more interested in the quality of his carvings than in the number of gimcracks he can turn out for the tourist trade."

Jenny backed into a parking space near the corner and stepped out of the car. In doing so, it was as if she had stepped into another world, or at least into a foreign country. Many of the older passers-by wore traditional Chinese trousers, loose overblouses, and little round black hats on their heads. A peculiar odor hung in the air. She wrinkled her nose when she realized that the smell came from a nearby store where rows of drying squid, eels, and other unsavory looking fish dangled on lines within reach of the customers.

"Ugh! I'm glad we won't have to go in there!" she laughed.

Dr. Avery, who had spent many years in the Orient, found nothing repulsive about the display.

"Those bins of ginger-root and other condiments are as familiar to a Chinese housewife as catsup and mustard are to American shoppers," he chuckled. "As for the dried octopus — well, different people regard different things as delicacies."

"I propose that we make a systematic search for our wood-carver," he added. "We may as well begin with this shop on the corner."

Paul and Jenny lingered for a moment to inspect the window display of brightly colored curios. By the time they entered the store Dr. Avery was already conversing with the proprietor.

"I'm positive this item wasn't sold here," the man declared. He returned the replica of the monkeys to the professor. "Most of our stock is imported from Hong Kong.

May I suggest an ivory fan for the young lady, or a box kite for the boy?"

Dr. Avery shook his head. "Not today, thank you. Just now it is essential that we find the person who made this carving. Do you know of a shop that carries this sort of merchandise?"

"No. It's out of our line," the man repeated, and turned to serve another customer.

This experience was duplicated dozens of times in the next few hours. By the time they had finished canvassing the fifth block, Jenny's feet ached, and she felt that she had seen enough silk scarves, jade ornaments, and hand-painted dishes to last her a lifetime.

Most of the little stores at which they inquired had various specialties, but as time passed she was struck by one distinct similarity.

"Have you noticed how many dragons are on display?" she asked. "Almost every place we've visited has had at least one picture or papier-mache figurine of a fire-breathing beast in sight. Why is that?"

"According to Chinese legend, the dragon is the god of thunder. *Lung*, as he is called there, supposedly forms clouds with his breath and thus provides rain to grow the rice crops," Dr. Avery explained. "This symbol is greatly honored by the Chinese people. Before the Communist government took over that country, they had celebrated a very colorful holiday called the Dragon Boat Festival. Out of respect for *Lung*, all the boats which participated in the regatta races were dragon-shaped. Nowadays, sad to say, such festitivites have been abolished."

The story interested Paul, and for a while he kept track of the number of dragons he spotted. Soon, however, he began complaining of hunger pangs.

Jenny squeezed his hand. "I'm feeling pretty hollow inside, myself," she admitted. "Maybe we could stop somewhere for a cup of tea and a plate of chow mein."

"You'll find more authentic food in this neighborhood," Dr. Avery laughed. "Chow mein and chop suey are American inventions. I see a cafe sign in the next block."

The restaurant's interior was dim and cool. A heady aroma of incense lingered above the cooking odors. Glancing around, Jenny saw that the spicy fragrance came from a smoldering pot in a wall niche. Behind it sat a small squat figure of the Buddha.

"This place certainly has atmosphere!" she exclaimed.

From the adjacent tables came a low singsong chatter of Cantonese. It was in this language that Dr. Avery addressed the waiter a few minutes later.

The man's round face broke into a grin of pleased surprise. He bowed low and answered the professor in the same musical tongue. In a short time he bustled back to place dishes of a delicious clear soup before them.

"Grandpa, what were you and that man saying?" Paul asked when the waiter had once more returned to the kitchen.

"We were only discussing the menu. He was delighted to meet an Occidental who spoke his native language," Dr. Avery explained. "I gathered that he and his family are refugees who fled from their homeland when the Communists came into power."

It was well past the noon hour, and most of the other customers had departed by the time the threesome finished their tasty meal. As a final touch, the waiter smilingly brought to their table a bowl of crisp fortune cookies. Paul and Jenny reached for them immediately, snapping open the wafer-thin pastry to remove the little slips of paper hidden inside.

But it was the bowl itself that attracted Dr. Avery's attention.

"No factory turned out this exquisite piece," he murmured, lifting the shallow wooden dish to examine it more carefully. "See the delicate chiseling on its sides? Someone devoted many hours to this intricate carving."

"Such work is a talent of my honorable father," declared the waiter proudly. "Long ago, he was famous in our province for his skill as an artisan, and he still makes a few things such as this to occupy his hands."

Jenny's pulse began to race with excitement. After hours of canvassing nearly every shop in Chinatown, she had almost despaired of ever finding the craftsman who had fashioned her treasured figurine. Was it possible that now, by the mere chance of Paul's appetite, they had stumbled at last on the right track?

With shaky fingers, she unwrapped Mark's present and held it toward the waiter. "Could you tell if this little carving was also made by your father?" she asked.

"To be sure." He nodded. "I would recognize his style anywhere. But how do you come to have this? As a rule, my father does not sell the things he makes, although he exhibits a few of them in that glass case near the window."

Dr. Avery answered for her. "The statuette was a gift to my young friend. Tell me," he added, "would it be possible for us to meet your father? The beauty of his carvings has given us much pleasure."

"I will be most happy to call him," the waiter agreed. He disappeared into the kitchen. Within a few minutes he returned. Hobbling along beside him was a very elderly gentleman whom he introduced as Soong Chi.

Looking up from his fortune cookies, Paul eyed the old man's silky white beard with fascination. Jenny reminded him of his manners with a nudge, and leaned forward anxiously as Dr. Avery and Soong Chi exchanged pleasantries in Cantonese. It was frustrating, she thought, not being able to understand a word they said!

It wasn't long, though, before their conversation turned to the statuette. The elderly craftsman beamed in recognition when he caught sight of the monkeys, and bobbed his head at some question from Dr. Avery.

When he had finished speaking, the professor interpreted his words for Jenny.

"Soong Chi remembers selling the figurine, and described the person who bought it," he said. "Two or three weeks ago a tall young man with black hair and eyes as blue as your own had lunch at this restaurant. He was dressed in ordinary seaman's clothes, and was accompanied by a couple of rough-looking companions. Later he returned here alone and persuaded Soong Chi to sell him the statue of the monkeys. That is the only time they saw him."

The story only added to Jenny's bewilderment. The physical details sounded like Mark, and yet — Her forehead puckered into a thoughtful frown. Ordinary seaman's clothes might serve as a useful disguise. Perhaps there was another reason, too, why her brother had adopted the outfit of a merchant mariner.

"Does Soong Chi recall whether the other two men were also dressed in sea clothes?" she asked.

When the question had been translated back and forth, Dr. Avery acknowledged that this was the case. "He makes them sound like a scurvy twosome," he added. "I'm afraid that, after all, tracing the statuette hasn't been of much help. The purchase was made weeks ago, and we don't know where your brother might have gone from here."

Jenny shook her head pensively. "Maybe we do. We're not far from the waterfront, are we?"

The waiter helpfully pointed out the fact that the docks were situated only a short distance away. Jenny smiled at him, and thanked the father and son for their assistance. When they had paid for their meal and were on their way back to the car, she explained her reasoning to the professor.

"Nothing will ever make me believe that Mark is a deserter," she said staunchly. "He must have a good reason for making friends with people who work around merchant vessels. If he's trying to gain their confidence, he'd be likely to dress as they do."

"And to go where they go," Dr. Avery agreed. "I suppose the waterfront is the most logical place for us to continue our search."

His tone sounded skeptical, though, and Jenny guessed that privately he felt their quest was useless. She was glad that he was too kind-hearted to say so aloud. Discouragement had a way of becoming contagious.

Before alighting from the car a second time, Jenny slipped on her sweater and helped Paul button his coat. Damp salt-smelling wisps of fog had begun billowing in along the long arm of the Bay, and already the Golden Gate Bridge was shrouded by the gray tentacles of mist. Without the gilding warmth of the sun's rays, the ramshackle buildings fringing the piers looked cheerless and forlorn.

"There're miles and miles of ships here, Jenny," Paul said, pointing to the rows of vessels riding at anchor in their moorings. "Are we going to hunt through all of them?"

"That would take weeks, I'm afraid. I hadn't bargained on there being so many docks," she admitted.

On some of the vessels sailors were busily hosing down the decks. Farther down the waterfront a crew of workers brushed new paint onto aging bulkheads, and in front of still other piers men were engaged in mending fishing nets.

"If we walk along here slowly, there is a chance you might recognize your brother," Dr. Avery suggested. "Even if the attempt doesn't succeed, you will know you've done your best to locate him."

Jenny flashed him a grateful smile and took Paul's chilly little hand as they started off. How lucky she was to have the Averys as her friends! She doubted whether she would have had the courage to saunter past these tough-looking crews alone.

A freighter at the upper end of the harbor was being loaded with cargo. The stevedores were apparently used to having spectators watch them while they worked, for they paid no attention to the threesome. Farther along, however, Jenny's searching gaze was belligerently returned by a group of bearded mariners. She walked a little faster, ignoring their insolent remarks, and pointed out the clock tower of the Ferry Building to Paul.

A few minutes later the old landmark had been completely blotted out by the ever-thickening fog. Even the click of their heels against the boardwalk sounded muffled and far away. Jenny's eyes smarted as she peered in turn at each bobbing vessel.

"Oh dear, this is hopeless! I can hardly see the superstructure on some of those ships," she groaned.

"In this pea soup I could pass six feet from Mark and never notice him!"

Dr. Avery turned his collar up to his ears. "I think it would be wisest if we turned back now. We should head for home while we can still find the way," he urged.

"All right," Jenny sighed, realizing that

unless they retraced their steps soon, they might not even be able to find their car.

With Paul trotting along beside her, she hurried back up the boardwalk. The wharf appeared to be almost deserted now. Most of the seamen had disappeared below deck, or found shelter within the dockside buildings.

They were not quite alone, however. Through the swirling mist she glimpsed a lone figure striding down the gangplank of a ship. She caught her breath, wondering if she had imagined that the set of his shoulders looked familiar. But there was something about the way he walked, too —

Jenny found herself running, stumbling ahead to catch up with the hurrying man. "Mark!" she called, certain now that she had not been mistaken. "Mark, it's me — Jenny!"

The man halted in mid-stride and swung toward her. The beginnings of an incredulous smile broke over his face. But before he could say a word, other footsteps thudded down the gangplank. The rumble of deep voices floated in their direction.

Mark's face tightened in alarm. He flung a desperate glance over his shoulder, then whirled back to Jenny.

"Put an ad in the paper," he ordered, in

tones barely loud enough for her to hear. "Let me know where I can reach you. Now get out of here — fast!"

It was a command, an urgent command, but for a moment Jenny was too stunned to move. She took a faltering step backward. As she did so, two villainous-looking seamen tramped across the boardwalk. Their eyes fastened suspiciously on her for an instant before they continued on to join Mark in the warehouse doorway.

The damp curtain of fog blotted out all but a few of their words, but her straining ears caught the mutter of a question. Mark's laughing voice drifted back to her.

"Crazy tourists . . . lost. . . ."

Not until a hand touched her elbow did she remember Dr. Avery and Paul. She blinked rapidly to hold back the tears as she regarded their sober faces.

"I found him!" she choked. "It *was* Mark. But he didn't want to talk to me. He said to get out of here in a hurry!"

Dr. Avery's grip managed to be gentle but forceful at the same time. "That *was* excellent advice," he murmured in a worried tone. "This is no place for you, Jenny. We'll take you home now."

A hundred questions babbled for attention inside her brain. Jenny couldn't find an answer to even one of them. Numbly, she moved on down the boardwalk. The fog was closing in quickly, shutting them off from everything and everyone. Heartsick and puzzled, she turned for a last look at the spot where Mark had last stood.

There was no trace of him — no trace of any living creature on the abandoned wharf. It was like a place in a dream — or a nightmare. Then, suddenly, for a split second, the fog cleared. Jenny realized that this particular spot wasn't quite anonymous, after all. There was a sign —

The letters wavered through the mist at her. Fuzzy as they were, she managed to read them. But identifying the sign hadn't made the situation any less perplexing. In fact, as she clutched Paul's fingers and headed back to the car she was feeling more confused than ever.

Why, she wondered frantically, had Mark been afraid to speak to her? And why, why, why, had he entered a warehouse belonging to the Marsh Shipping Lines?

# Chapter Nine

It took a good night's sleep to make Jenny see things in perspective again. Reviewing the scene on the wharf, she realized that by blundering into Mark she might have made things very difficult for him. It wasn't, she decided, that he hadn't wanted to speak to her. Obviously, he had been afraid to stop and talk just then — afraid for both her and himself. More than ever, she was convinced that he was working under cover. For what reason she couldn't begin to guess. But she had no doubt that those two cutthroats who had joined him were part of the plot!

Jenny gulped, glad that Mark had had the quick wittedness to pass her and the Averys off as tourists. She hoped the explanation had satisfied them. Still, she couldn't shrug off the sensation of impending danger. Just seeing her brother in the company of those two men had increased her uneasiness about his safety.

Throwing back the covers, she wondered again about the building she had watched them enter. Was it only coincidence that had taken Mark and his companions into a warehouse belonging to the Marsh Shipping Lines? Or was it possible that in some way he was mixed up in the piracy plaguing that company's ships?

With a sigh, she gave up trying to puzzle it out. Mark would explain when he got the chance. All she could do until then was keep on believing in him.

On the way home from church Dr. Avery suddenly remembered that they had been invited to attend a barbecue at the Wynnes' home that afternoon.

"Mrs. Wynne is especially anxious to meet you," he told Miss Ursula. "And I understand that they have a small son who is just Paul's age. We should all have a most relaxing time."

Jenny excused herself from accompanying them to the barbecue, delightful as it sounded; she enjoyed living with the Averys and being accepted as practically one of their family. Nevertheless, she felt self-conscious about intruding in their affairs.

Besides, she reminded herself, there was something important she had to do. It couldn't be postponed another minute.

As soon as they had left she hurried into the study. Snatching up pencil and notepad, she seated herself at the desk. What was it Mark had said? "Put an ad in the paper. Let me know where I can reach you . . ."

After considerable thought, Jenny decided on the wording of her message. It had to be clear enough for her brother to understand, yet incomprehensible to others who might chance across it. She reread the wording a final time and nodded in satisfaction. It ought to confuse nearly everyone!

"Mark: Monkeys received. I believe no evil. Call me in Monterey at . . ."

Her phone number and name followed.

Mark hadn't mentioned which paper, Jenny recalled. To make sure of having it reach him, she telephoned both major San Francisco newspapers and asked that the message be placed in the "Personals" column of their want-ads section as quickly as possible. After inquiring about their charges, she typed out duplicate confirmation copies of the ad, wrote checks in the amounts requested, and addressed envelopes to the *Chronicle* and to the *Examiner.*

"Oh, glory, I hope this works," she

fretted. "If I don't find out what Mark is up to soon, I may join the merchant marine myself!"

She stuck stamps on the envelopes and hurried uphill to the mailbox, which was situated halfway between their house and the Briswalds' property.

It was a heavenly day, warm and a little breezy. Not a wisp of the previous evening's fog lingered in the air. Turning away from the mailbox, Jenny felt a pang of regret that she hadn't, after all, accompanied the Averys to the barbecue. It would have been fun —

"Hi there, Jenny!"

She jerked her head up in surprise, then waved as she caught sight of Van Gilbert. With a happy grin, he nosed his shiny blue convertible toward the curb.

"Walking! I should have guessed you were an outdoor girl. I'm surprised you aren't getting your exercise in the Wynnes' swimming pool today."

"Aren't there any secrets in this town?" Jenny laughed. "Monterey reminds me of a party line — everyone knows what's going on!"

"Oh, that's only among the Center group," Van chuckled. "Besides, I was invited too. One day a week, though, I prefer to get away from crowds. I'm going to take my sailboat out for a spin. Like to come along?"

Jenny hesitated, glancing down at the neat gray suit she had worn to church. "Sure I wouldn't count as a crowd?"

"No chance of that. The *Hurricane Edna* has room for only two people aboard. Cozy." Dubiously, Van shook his head at Jenny's Sunday apparel. "You'll need sneakers and slacks and a warm windbreaker. I have an errand to do for my uncle first, but I'll pick you up in half an hour. Your chunk of beach."

Giving her no time to answer, he gunned his motor. With a deft spin of the wheel, he pulled back out on the street and zoomed down the hill. In less than a minute the speeding convertible was out of sight.

Heavens! I hope he doesn't sail as fast as he drives! Jenny giggled to herself.

She hadn't definitely agreed to go; but hurrying back up the walk, she realized that she was looking forward to the excursion. Just a short time earlier she had been regretting the missed barbecue, but a sail would be even more amusing than that had promised to be.

After all, she and Van had been properly introduced at Dr. Wynne's party. He was certainly a personable young man. Hard-working, too, she thought, racing upstairs to fling on sports clothes. Even his Sundays were partially taken up by errands for Hammond Marsh.

Fifteen minutes of her alloted half hour still remained when she had finished changing. Not time enough to put together a picnic lunch to measure up to Miss Ursula's high standards, but sufficient leeway to make sure they wouldn't go hungry.

Moving at top speed, Jenny concocted sandwiches out of cold cuts, sliced two healthy slabs of the chocolate cake from last night's dessert, and filled a thermos to the brim with lemonade and ice cubes.

All this fit nicely into a large paper bag. Jenny rolled down the top of it to prevent the edges from flapping in the wind, then slipped out the back door. Just as she reached the gated fence that led onto the beach she caught sight of a tiny boat tacking gracefully down the shoreline.

Skillfully, Van headed the little craft closer and closer toward land. Jenny hopped aboard the instant its keel touched the low-tide mark on the sand. Van gave her a hand up; then, with the assistance of his outboard motor, he maneuvered the boat out of the shallows.

"That's not really cricket," he admitted, flipping off the engine switch. "Real sailing enthusiasts look with scorn on any sort of power that isn't supplied by the wind. But a little extra thrust is mighty handy to have around at times." He eyes the paper sack with interest. "Don't tell me you brought your own life preserver!"

"In a way. Provisions. Mighty handy to have around at times," Jenny good-naturedly mimicked his sentiments.

After a peek at the food, Van stowed the bag under a tarpaulin, where it wouldn't become soaked by the spray. "I can see that I invited the right girl along," he said approvingly. "Anywhere special you'd like to go?"

"No, just let *Hurricane Edna* have her head." Jenny leaned back, letting the salty breeze ruffle her hair. "It's a darling little boat. Why did you give her such an odd name?"

Van eased the rudder back, expertly guiding the sailboat out into the open sea. "She's named after the first storm I ever charted," he explained. "I got interested in meteorology when I was stationed in the Caribbean with the Coast Guard. Used to do a lot of weather projecting on my own, just for practice. When a violent storm blew up without warning one night, I was the first one to track the eye. It was a frightening experience, but thrilling, too."

"I can well imagine!"

Keeping the *Hurricane Edna* scudding smoothly along occupied most of Van's attention for the next hour or so. With nothing to do but relax and enjoy the cruise, Jenny's thoughts reverted to the crisis facing the Center. Loyalty to his uncle might keep Van silent regarding Hammond Marsh's future plans. But being so close to the matter, it was possible he had a theory about the pirates that she hadn't heard yet.

"I still find it hard to think of piracy existing in the twentieth century," she remarked. "They must be a daring lot. Everyone is dreadfully concerned that the attacks may continue."

"Especially Uncle Hammond!" Van fervently agreed. "Any mention of those marauders brings his blood pressure up to the boiling point. He believes their assaults are a personal insult to him and the company. I don't see it that way myself. It stands to reason that the Center's cargoes are hijacked because they're so much more valuable than the loads carried by regular freighters."

His opinion made sense to Jenny. "With the United States Navy in on the search, it's a wonder that the pirate ship hasn't been spotted long before this," she mused. "Even considering California's tremendous stretch of coastline, somebody must have seen her."

"If so, they're keeping it a deep, dark secret," Van declared morosely.

There had been a sharp breeze when they first started out, but for several minutes the impact of wind against the boat's sails had been lessening. Since it seemed temporarily becalmed, Van decided that it was a good time for lunch. He poured the lemonade into paper cups while Jenny doled out sandwiches and cake.

"If the *Hurricane Edna* had room for a galley, I'd sign you on as cook," he complimented her.

"Thanks, Skipper. I'll keep your recommendation in mind, next time I go looking for a job," Jenny laughed. "Meanwhile, I suppose we had better be getting back. I wouldn't want the professor or Miss Ursula to worry if they found me missing when they return."

With the help of his motor, Van got the sailboat headed back toward shore. They had been farther out than Jenny realized, and she found the view from the sea side of the coast both beautiful and interesting.

"Is that your house? On the very top of the cliff?" She pointed as they neared the rocky shore.

"Yes. In his younger days Uncle Hammond used to spend a lot of time watching the ships steam back and forth," Van said. "He misses the view since he's been confined to his wheelchair — those large windows are on the top floor. Nowadays our neighbor seems to do most of the watching."

"Mr. Briswald?" Shading her eyes from the glare, Jenny saw that his was the only home that stood between Avery's house and Hammond Marsh's hilltop residence. "Paul and I caught sight of him the other day — or rather he caught sight of us. Through a spyglass! Why on earth has he fenced off his beach?"

Van shrugged. "Briswald's a peculiar old coot. Never sets foot out the door in the daytime, but he knows what is going on around here, all right. If you ask me, there's something fishy about him. I wouldn't be surprised —"

"Surprised at what?" Jenny asked when he paused.

Van's dark eyes twinkled conspiringly. "It's probably slanderous, what I'm thinking," he admitted, "but more than once I've wondered whether he might not be the pirates' spotter! He's in a perfect location to survey the entire harbor. All he has to do is watch — and make a phone call at the proper time."

Jenny gasped. "Does the Coast Guard know about this?"

"What could they do? There's no proof," Van grumbled. "But I won't be satisfied until I learn a lot more about our mysterious neighbor!"

It was on the tip of Jenny's tongue to mention the perplexing letter Mrs. Briswald had dropped, the letter addressed to "Captain Amos Bohling" but which bore the Briswalds' address.

At that moment, however, a violent gust of wind buffeted the *Hurricane Edna*'s sails. Van threw his entire weight on the rudder and executed a tricky maneuver to keep the tiny craft from capsizing. Even so, her keel brushed perilously close to a jagged outcropping of rock. Jenny, holding her breath, promptly forgot about the other incident.

She managed a shaky smile for Van when he beached the boat and held her steady while she hopped out onto the sand.

"That was a grand display of seamanship! For a minute there, I had visions of plunging straight down to Davy Jones's locker!" She held out her hand for the thermos. "Thanks again for a glorious afternoon!"

When he had shoved off, she took a couple of deep breaths to steady her rubbery knees. She was still crossing the sand when two figures hurtled through the gate and thudded down to meet her.

"Jenny, we were watching! Are you all right?" Paul cried.

Russ MacAllister gave her no chance to answer. "What were you trying to do — get yourself killed?" he demanded gruffly.

"Certainly not!" Jenny retorted. "Van handled the boat like a pro. A sudden blast of wind threw him off balance for a minute, that's all. Besides, we weren't very far out. We could have swum ashore."

Russ cast an angry look at the retreating sailboat. "Not if you'd been dashed against those rocks, you couldn't! They'd have cut you to ribbons!"

It suddenly occurred to Jenny that Russ was irate only because he had been so worried. She beamed a peace-making smile at the sandy-haired young man.

"It *was* a close call," she admitted. "Thanks for being so concerned, but really, I'm quite all right."

Russ hid his relief behind a quip. "You'd better be! Dr. Avery invited me back here for dinner with the family, after which we're going to tackle a few more basic nouns and verbs in Hindi. I'm counting on you to help me with my homework."

Several hours later, Jenny learned that he had meant exactly what he said. He was in deadly earnest about his mission to help the Indian farmers, and he was determined to be able to communicate adequately in their language before he sailed.

"Let me say these words back to you a few times," Russ requested when his short session with the professor had ended. "I could memorize them all right by staring at the paper, but the accent is the important part."

Jenny led him to a quiet spot in the living room where they could practice undisturbed. Russ tackled his assignment so diligently that at last she was forced to call a halt.

"If we go over them one more time, we'll both be reciting in our sleep," she laughed. "I may wind up learning another language secondhand!"

Russ closed his book and apologized. "Sorry if I tired you out."

"You haven't — not a bit. I'll be delighted to review your lessons with you as often as you can come," Jenny assured him. "I only wish there was more I could do to help the Center. If I'd had the sense to train as a nurse instead of a librarian, I would volunteer for an Asian assignment myself."

"A librarian, eh?" A speculative look came over Russ's face. "Maybe there is something you could do. The people of rural India aren't illiterate by any means, but their educational program hasn't caught up with that of the big cities yet. If you could collect a box or two of books to send over with us, we might be able to do a little teaching in our spare time."

"Why, that's a wonderful idea!" Jenny applauded. "There are dozens of libraries in the Bay Area. I imagine most of them would be willing to contribute a few extra books to such a worthy cause!"

By the time Russ left to return to his boarding house, she had already thought of several practical ways to bolster their plan. Almost dancing with excitement, she said good night to the professor and Miss Ursula and tripped upstairs to get ready for bed.

But even after she had bathed, and brushed her hair a hundred strokes, she was still far too elated to feel like sleeping. Trying to decide what type of books the volunteers would find most useful, she wandered over to the sliding glass door that opened onto the balcony.

Jenny stepped out, reveling in the air's salty tang. The night was still, but not completely silent. Small white-capped breakers hurled themselves against the shore with bubbling sighs before receding into the ocean to renew their force. It looked absolutely peaceful and serene. Remembering the afternoon's adventure in Van's sailboat, though, Jenny knew that the sea could be treacherous, too.

She stood there staring out at the churning depths, her mind busy with plans for the book collection. Thus preoccupied with her thoughts, it was only gradually that she became aware of the shadow darkening the waves. Not until it slid within wading distance of the shore did Jenny snap out of her trance and realize abruptly that the long, dark shape was a boat.

She gaped at it, utterly astonished. Its dim running lights wavered, then snapped suddenly out. For a moment Jenny felt sure that the vessel had run aground and become stranded on the beach.

But when she peered again at the spot where the craft had last been sighted, the filtering moonlight showed only foaming water whispering against the sand.

Nowhere along that deserted stretch of shoreline was there the slightest sign that the boat had ever existed!

# Chapter Ten

There had been a boat. She was sure of it! But where could it have gone?

Jenny took a firm grip on the wrought-iron balcony. Balancing precariously on her toes, she leaned out as far as she could. The fence on the near side of the Briswalds' property was clearly visible in the moonlight. Incredulously, she scanned the fifteen or twenty yards of shoreline extending past the barrier. Not so much as a sand crab moved on the quiet beach.

That blasted cliff is in my way! she fumed, wishing fervently that the bulging hillside did not obscure her view of their neighbor's land.

There was no mistaking that the boat had headed straight in toward the beach. No sailor would have ventured so close to the shallows unless he meant to dock fairly close by.

Or unless he intended to pick up someone along the shore, Jenny thought. But even the swiftest operation of that sort would have taken at least a minute. Yet only seconds had intervened from the time she spotted the craft and the moment it had mysteriously vanished from sight.

It could, she conceded, have turned at the last minute and continued along the shore, past the Marsh's frontage and around the point. But then why had its running lights flickered out — even before the dark hulking shadow had disappeared?

With a shiver that had nothing to do with the balmy night breeze, she remembered Van voicing his suspicions of their taciturn neighbor. Was it really possible that the man next door was mixed up in some shady business — perhaps even involved in the hijacking of the Center's cargoes?

"I don't see why not," she murmured. "Criminals have to live somewhere. And that was a pretty large boat!"

Still, although she had focused on it for only an instant, she doubted that the craft she had seen was big enough to have been the pirate ship. It had looked more like a good-sized cabin cruiser, while Elaine Kendall had termed the marauders' vessel a "speedy cutter." Which might, of course, have only been her way of describing it.

Unconvinced, Jenny shook her head. The pirate ship was heavily armed.

Besides, it would need a huge space on deck and in the hold to accommodate those tons of stolen machinery and other goods. No cabin cruiser, regardless of size, had that kind of room aboard.

But this logical conclusion in no way lessened her distrust of Mr. Briswald. There was no reason why the pirates couldn't own a smaller boat, too, and it was toward his beach that the craft had headed. Possibly at this very moment it was anchored just out of her range of vision, on the far side of his property.

She cast a final searching glance at the deserted shoreline. There was nothing further to be learned from her balcony. As she turned to reenter her bedroom, though, a possible solution to the enigma occurred to her. There were lots of tiny channels and inlets all along the coast. Maybe one of them twisted into the Briswalds' stretch of beach. It wouldn't have to be very wide or very deep — just roomy enough to float a cruiser. The boat could even be kept there permanently, hidden by some garagelike device.

"I'll investigate first thing tomorrow," Jenny decided aloud, snuggling into her covers. "Fence or no fence, he can't prevent me from swimming past his beach.

You can't barricade a whole ocean!"

But the following morning something happened to delay her ambitious plan. At breakfast, she mentioned Russ's suggestion to Dr. Avery. The professor enthusiastically seconded the idea and encouraged her to present it to Dr. Wynne for his approval.

"Come down to the Center with me this morning. Talk it over with him," he urged. "Most likely he will have some pertinent recommendations. Then, too, he could supply you with a letter to the libraries, which would strengthen your chances of getting donations from them."

Miss Ursula, her perky white head cocked to one side, had been listening to their discussion.

"I think it's wonderful that you have found an outside interest, Jenny. Lately you've been spending far too much time shut up here at home with Paul and me."

"I wouldn't call it being shut up," Jenny laughed. "Anyway, didn't you ask me to come north with you to help out?"

"Nonsense!" said Miss Ursula firmly. "My arthritis has hardly given me a twinge since we arrived. Furthermore, you're spoiling me by taking over so much of the housework. We enjoy having you live here, my dear, but we have no intention of allowing you to become a servant!"

Jenny was touched by their obvious affection for her. "In that case, I had better make myself useful in some other day," she declared. "Come on, Dr. Avery, I'll drive you to class."

Luckily, they found the director in his office. A bit hesitantly, Jenny mentioned the book-collecting plan to him, giving Russell MacAllister credit for having originated the idea.

"Russ thought that since I'd had library training, I would be able to choose some worthwhile books for use in the field," she said. "I don't know how successful I'll be —"

"Who could resist such a sincere appeal?" Dr. Wynne laughed. "All sorts of organizations, and private citizens, too, have offered to help in our work. I'm sure you will find many people willing to assist you."

His words gave Jenny another idea. "Besides the libraries, the general public might have some books they wish to donate. They wouldn't necessarily have to be in a foreign language, either. Don't many Asiatics speak English?"

"Certainly." He nodded. "Especially in

India. Because of the long British protectorship of that country, English has become almost a second native language there." He ticked some subjects off on his fingers. "Children's story book, texts, how-to-do-it volumes — the list of useful titles is practically endless."

Jenny smiled, relieved at having won his wholehearted approval. "Then, if you don't object, I'll insert an ad in the local paper asking for donations. The people can bring their books here to the Center, and I will be happy to do all the sorting. In the meantime, I'll start canvassing the community libraries."

The director called in his secretary and dictated a letter endorsing Jenny's activities on behalf of the Center. "Good luck," he said, signing it with a flourish.

Jenny tucked the letter in her purse. Dr. Avery had already given her permission to use the car. Intent on her errand, she headed for the door. But as she crossed the reception room she turned in response to a friendly hail.

"Remember me?" Deedee Jay asked shyly.

"Of course. It's nice to see you again." Jenny detoured over to the coffee machine where the pony-tailed girl stood. To be companionable, she poured herself a cup.

"Are you getting oriented for your trip to the Orient?" she joked.

Deedee held up a thick textbook on the Hindi language. "Doing my best. Our class starts in half an hour. I brought this out here to 'cram' while Bruce is having a dentistry lesson. Poor fellow," she added sympathetically. "He's having to unlearn all the modern techniques and practice doing things manually again. The up to-date dentistry equipment weighs far too much to bring along with us."

Jenny carried her coffee over to a nearby table and sat down beside Deedee. "Russ is learning Hindi, too," she said. "Will you and Bruce be assigned to the same area where he is posted?"

"Yes, and I'm so glad. It's bound to be lonely at first," Deedee said. "I imagine it will be difficult, adjusting to a new way of life. But we'll probably all be too busy to notice. Fortunately, I trained as a dental assistant, so I'll be right there in the clinic with Bruce most of the time."

"That sounds positively blissful. Two hearts beating as one while the cavities are repaired!" Jenny laughed, aware that the young couple had been married only a few months.

She finished the last of her coffee, then pushed back her chair. "I'd better let you get back to your studies. Let's try to get together again soon."

Before walking out to the car, Jenny looked up the address of the nearest library. There she was warmly welcomed by the staff when she explained her errand. The superintendent promised to take the matter up with his colleagues at their next weekly meeting.

"We have multiple copies of a great many books," he told her. "I am certain no one will object if we give some of them to the Center. I'll see to it myself, and I'll have the volumes delivered within a month."

"Thank you so much." Jenny beamed. "Dr. Wynne and the volunteers will be most grateful."

There were two other libraries in the vicinity, and she managed a short visit to each of them that morning. At both places she was given the same cordial reception. Returning home, she felt a glow of satisfaction. The campaign was off to a good start!

Lunch was waiting for her when she arrived home. After they had eaten, she cleared the table and coaxed Miss Ursula into taking a rest. "I'll entertain Paul this afternoon," she promised.

While washing the dishes, Jenny's thoughts reverted to the book-collecting program. An ad in the local paper still sounded like a good idea. But maybe there was an even better way than calling people's attention to the plan. Most of the neighborhood grocery stores had bulletin boards. Why not tack up a notice on each of these, asking for donations?

But there was no time to type out the appeals just then. Paul waited until she set aside the dish towel, then turned a couple of cartwheels across the kitchen floor to attract her attention.

"I'm waiting to be entertained," he hinted solemnly. "It's a nice warm day, Jenny. Can't we go for that swim you promised me last week?"

"Your memory would put an elephant's to shame!" she laughed. "Oh, all right. Let's go put on our swimsuits. But I think that water must come down from Siberia. Don't blame me if you turn blue!"

Tiptoeing up the stairs so as not to wake Miss Ursula, Jenny suddenly remembered that Paul's eagerness for a swim coincided with her own plans. Now was a perfect time to make a thorough investigation of Mr. Briswald's beach!

Paul hadn't exaggerated about the weather. The temperature had been mounting all morning, and now must be close to 90°, Jenny decided. Hand in hand, they crossed the sand at a run to avoid scorching their feet, but she pulled him back before his toes touched the water.

"Not so fast there, frogman! It's only been half an hour since we've eaten. Why don't you build a sand castle while your lunch settles?"

"Okay. You build one, too. Bet mine is bigger than yours!"

Tunneling in the damp sand was a pleasant way to use up the minutes. Paul kept casting wistful glances at the rolling surf, however, and Jenny also found it hard to control her impetuosity.

While fidgeting the time away, she wondered whether she could have imagined last night's incident. Had that ghostlike cabin cruiser really coasted in toward shore — or had the whole thing been a mirage caused by eerie shadows flickering across the waves? She didn't think she had been mistaken — but there was only one way to find out!

Unable to bear the suspense any longer, Jenny leaped up and bounded into the frothing surf. Paul darted after her. He plunged headlong into the first breaker that crested against the shore.

The water was still briskly cool, Jenny thought, but at least this time it wasn't quite like jumping into a tray of ice cubes!

She splashed a handful of foam at the little boy and ducked under the waves, coming up a good ten feet nearer the fence. She kept her eyes averted from the stretch of windows at the rear of the Briswald house. Even so, the thought of that spyglass gave her a prickly feeling. Probably it was trained on them now, magnifying their every movement!

Paul seemed to have forgotten about the watchful form in the window, for he followed her lead without a trace of apprehension. Within a few minutes they were on a direct line with the barricaded beach.

With only her head above water. Jenny couldn't see what lay beyond the mounded sand. Still pretending to be merely playful, she flipped over on her stomach. A dozen swift strokes gave her the answer she sought.

A shallow inlet, four or five feet in width, hooked into the beach. It snaked its way right to the base of the sloping hill on which the house was built — but that was all. Solid rock turned back the water at that point. There was no small dock, such as Jenny had pictured in her speculations of the night before. No "garage" in which a boat could be secretly moored. Nothing except an innocent little channel detouring in from the coastline — and out again.

Jenny didn't know whether to feel disappointed or relieved. No boat larger than a canoe could slide up that shallow creek without scraping bottom. Obviously, this hadn't been the destination of the cabin cruiser she had spotted from her balcony. It must have been headed somewhere else — *if* it had been solid and not shadow, real and not imagined.

But where?

Paul splashed up alongside her. "You aren't tired already, are you? I'll race you to those rocks at the end of our beach!"

He spurted ahead, not seeing the flash of light that glinted for a moment behind the windows of the silent house far above. The brilliant glare hit Jenny's eyes, though. She threw one last puzzled look at the narrow inlet, then churned after Paul. Mr. Briswald was still as much of a riddle as ever. She was right back where she had started!

Russ telephoned her that evening.

Pleased to hear his voice, Jenny reported her first successful efforts at following through on his suggestion.

"You'll soon have books enough for a traveling library of your own," she declared optimistically. "How are your lessons coming?"

"Fine. Would you like to give me a hand with them again tomorrow?"

Jenny promptly agreed. She considered discussing her suspicions of their unneighborly neighbor with him, but when Russ mentioned that he was wading through a tome on the Indian caste system, she decided that he had enough on his mind. Van Gilbert would be the logical confidant, she thought. He, too, distrusted Mr. Briswald. If only they could find some link between the pirates and that dour coast-watcher!

Before going up to bed, she borrowed a textbook on the Hindi language from Dr. Avery. She could help Russ better, she reasoned, if she had some notion of the spelling and pronunciation of the words he was learning.

"I've heard that there are many different dialects spoken in India," she said. "Won't the volunteers have trouble communicating if they are transferred from one province to another?"

"Not nowadays," the professor explained. "It used to be most difficult — as many as fifteen or twenty major languages were spoken in that country. But after the war, when the British left and the Indians took over their own government, the people decided that it would be simpler to adopt one official language. They settled on Hindi, which is a variant of Hindustani. Between that and English, a traveler should have no problem making himself understood anywhere in India."

"I'm glad of that." Jenny smiled. "Russ and the others will probably be far too busy to learn fifteen languages!"

During the next few days she visited half a dozen branch libraries, posted an appeal for books in every grocery store in town, and spent two evenings studying with Russ. She found that the hours almost flew by when they were together. On Friday morning he waylaid her as she was leaving the Center.

"I think we've earned a night off," he said. "How about taking in a movie this evening? Deedee and Bruce are going. We could make it a foursome."

"It sounds like fun," Jenny agreed.

"Fine. I'll pick you up at seven."

They found a good comedy playing at one of the downtown theatres. After the show the two couples dropped in at a vintage cafe near Fisherman's Wharf and indulged in a late snack. Everyone talked and laughed a great deal.

When Russ and Bruce got up to drop more coins in the jukebox, Deedee gazed around the cozy diner with a trace of sadness. "I guess this is what I'll miss most when I'm far from home," she sighed. "Having a girl friend to giggle with, and looking forward to an evening out once in a while."

"Think of it as being a two-year honeymoon," Jenny suggested. "The time spent overseas will be an experience you and Bruce can look back on with pride all your lives."

"I know it will be worthwhile — and probably not nearly so dreary as I'm picturing it." Deedee smiled shyly. "Please don't think I regret our decision. I'd be sorry if we didn't have this chance to do something for others."

The boys returned before Jenny could reply, but she remembered Deedee's words for a long time afterward. In a small way she too was sharing in the work. She only wished she were going with them!

Getting out of the little Volkswagen half an hour later, she thanked Russ for an enjoyable evening. "I had a wonderful time. Maybe we can all get together for a picnic or something one day soon," she said, including Bruce and Deedee in her good nights.

As she unlatched the front door she reflected that August was not very far away. Before long, they would all be leaving —

The shrill of the telephone broke into her thoughts. Hurrying to silence it before the noise woke the Averys, she snatched up the receiver.

"Jenny?" said a familiar voice in her ear. "I've got to talk to you. Can you meet me — someplace where it's not too public?"

# Chapter Eleven

Jenny caught her breath and clutched at the table to steady her sagging knees. "Mark! Mark, is it really you?"

"None other. 'Home is the sailor, home from the sea —' " He broke off, adding hastily, "Listen, Sis, I haven't much time. My two ugly pals may show up any minute."

"Those awful men I saw you with on Saturday?" Jenny struggled to keep the tremor out of her voice. "Can't you get away from them? Are they holding you prisoner?"

"You've got it the wrong way 'round," Mark chuckled. "I'm trying my best not to let them get away from me!" His tone faded out for an instant, as though he had whirled around to look over his shoulder. "There isn't time to explain anything now. But it's vital that I talk with you — especially since you've somehow gotten mixed up with that crowd from the Center. Can you think of a place to meet where no one is likely to see us?"

"There's an ice-cream parlor not far from here. It stays open till all hours on weekends."

"Good enough. Wait for me there between nine-thirty and ten tomorrow night."

There was a sudden click as the connection was broken. Jenny stared for a long, tense moment at the dead receiver before setting the phone back in its cradle. Far from reassuring her as to his safety, Mark's call had left her feeling more alarmed than ever.

Mystified, she reflected that her brother hadn't asked for the address of the ice-cream store. That must mean that he was familiar with this neighborhood. She had included only her phone number in the ad, but somehow he had discovered exactly where she was living.

Even more baffling than this was his curt reference to "that crowd from the Center." Jenny wondered distraughtly what Mark had learned about the organization. It seemed to be promoting such wonderful work. There couldn't be anything sinister about Dr. Wynne and his staff — could there be?

Dread clutched at her heart. Resolutely, she pushed the oppressive feeling away.

Mark couldn't possibly suspect those dedicated men of wrongdoing, she told herself. She must have misunderstood him!

Nevertheless, it was hours before she finally fell into a restless sleep. Her dreams were haunted by fleeting glimpses of dark, shadowy ships and unrecognizable men wearing eye patches.

Jenny awoke to a wind-tossed Saturday morning. Immediately her worries of the night before returned. She still couldn't convince herself that the Center was anything more than it appeared to be. But there was always that possibility. And if it were true, Russ, Deedee, Bruce — all her new friends — might be heading for terrible danger.

Fortunately, there was enough housework to prevent her from brooding too much during the morning hours. After lunch, Dr. Avery drove Miss Ursula to a meeting of the local garden club, which she had been invited to join. Jenny was left in charge of Paul.

"Want to help me make cookies?" she asked, hoping to keep him inside on such a blustery day.

"Well — for a little while, maybe," he agreed. "I planned on doing something else later on."

Jenny was rummaging in the cupboard for cookie cutters and didn't pay much attention to his remark.

"Can't find a one," she reported, climbing down from the stool. "But that's okay. I've thought of something even better."

With scissors and cardboard, she fashioned the pattern of a gingerbread man. After she had finished rolling out the dough, Paul painstakingly traced around the outline with a blunt knife.

"Um, there'll be plenty for everyone here. We can dress them up with icing after they're baked," Jenny proposed, transferring the gingerbread men to a cookie sheet.

Just as she was popping them into the oven, the doorbell rang.

"Hi! Come on in," she greeted Van Gilbert. "Are you the fellow we blame for this nasty weather?"

"Doesn't everyone? That's one of the fringe detractions of my job," the handsome young meteorologist joked ruefully.

"Then, to be fair, I'll call you up to say thanks next time we get a nice day," Jenny promised. She led the way into the kitchen. "Paul and I have been making cookies — Heavens, where did he go?"

She looked around and called his name, but there was no answer.

"Oh, quit worrying." Van shrugged. "You know how kids are. Always running off on some project of their own."

"He did mention that there was something else he'd planned on doing," Jenny recalled. Puzzled, she walked over to the window. There was no sign of the active eight-year-old in the yard.

She turned back to Van, assuming that Paul had gone to his room to play. "Has there been any further news about the masked marauders?"

"No, worse luck." He grimaced. "To hear my uncle carry on, you'd think that piracy was invented specifically to harass him! But I didn't come over to talk about that. I was hoping to persuade you to sign on for another cruise aboard the *Hurricane Edna*. Tomorrow afternoon?"

Jenny hesitated. Much as she had enjoyed her first sailboat ride, she couldn't help recalling the near-tragic climax it had had. And in this sort of weather —

"Aren't rain squalls predicted for tonight and tomorrow?" she hedged.

"Nothing serious. It should be clear by noon." Van helped himself to a still-warm gingerbread man, and smiled coaxingly at her. "This time I'll even bring the lunch!"

"All right — provided it's not too windy. One o'clock at the beach?"

This arrangement suited Van. A few minutes later he left, promising to see her the next day.

When his footsteps had faded away down the walk, Jenny paused in the hall with a growing sense of uneasiness. The house seemed much too quiet. On an impulse, she hurried up the stairs and into Paul's room.

Except for the furniture, it was completely empty.

Really beginning to worry now, Jenny darted back down the stairs. There was only one other place Paul could have gone to!

She flew through the kitchen and out the back door. One glance was enough to tell her that he wasn't in the garden. She sprinted down the terraced slope to the gate, anxiously scanning the churning surf.

"Paul! Paul, where are you?"

Jenny was halfway across the sand when a small head bobbed into view thirty yards down the shoreline. She gasped and ran toward him as the boy struggled onto the beach.

"You little scamp! You frightened me half out of my wits!" she scolded. "Don't you know better than to go swimming without me? Some of those waves are higher than you are!"

"I waited till a whole hour after lunch. Just like you always told me to," Paul retorted defensively.

He was shivering with the cold, and too tuckered out to do much talking. Eyeing him as they hurried back to the house, Jenny felt her suspicions rise.

"What were you doing down in that direction, anyway?"

"I kept thinking about the bad man," Paul muttered. "He didn't have any reason to chase me away before. Jenny, there's something awfully funny —"

"Before! Then this isn't the first time you've gone swimming on your own?" Fear of what might easily have happened to her small charge sharpened Jenny's tone. She grabbed a towel and began drying him energetically. After a moment she stooped down and spoke to him in a softer voice.

"Honey, try to understand. I'm not mad — only scared that you might drown or get tossed against the rocks. Or stir up trouble with our neighbor. He isn't the friendliest man in the world, you know." She gave him a forgiving hug. "Promise me you won't stick even a toe into the water again unless

I'm right there with you."

"Okay. But Jenny —"

She hustled him up the stairs and helped him into warm, dry clothing. "No 'but Jennies!' Think how terrible your grandfather and Aunt Ursula would feel if you were injured. And I would, too. So let's not talk about it any more. Come on back to the kitchen and we'll finish decorating the gingerbread men."

Obediently, Paul trotted downstairs behind her. He didn't mention swimming or the "bad man" again. But it was quite a while before the speculative frown left his round, earnest face. Then suddenly he nodded to himself and broke into a satisfied smile. Unfortunately, at that moment Jenny was busy with the frosting. Otherwise, she might have guessed from his expression that he had thought of a new idea.

The rain squalls predicted by Van and his fellow weathermen arrived right on schedule. Even with the afternoon's excitement, the hours had dragged by for Jenny. It seemed that the time for her meeting with Mark would never arrive! At nine o'clock, unable to sit still for an instant longer, she pulled on her raincoat and knotted a scarf around her short black hair.

"I'm going to take a hike down to the ice-cream store," she told Dr. Avery and Miss Ursula. "Want me to bring you back some rocky road?"

The professor, lost in a book, declined absently. "Not for me, thank you," Miss Ursula said, looking up from her mending. She frowned in concern as a blast of wind rattled the house. "Are you sure you'll be warm enough? Take the car if you'd rather not walk in this rain."

"A little damp fresh air won't hurt me," Jenny answered politely. "The shop is just down at the foot of the hill. I'll be back in an hour or so."

When the front door had closed behind her, she shoved her hands deep in her pockets and bent her head against the wind. All day she had felt twinges of conscience for not having told the Averys about Mark's call, or not mentioning the appointment she had made to meet him. But her brother's mysterious reference to the Center had kept her silent. Until she learned exactly what Mark had meant, she thought it wisest to avoid all discussion of him.

She was thoroughly wet by the time she

arrived at the soda shop. A freckled youth stood behind the counter polishing glasses. She looked past him anxiously and felt a spark of disappointment when she saw that only one table was occupied. Four teen-agers, just shrugging into their coats, were the ice-cream parlor's lone customers.

Jenny waited until they had paid their bill, then ordered a chocolate milk shake.

"Okay if I take it over to one of the tables?" she asked, handing the soda jerk some coins. "I'm waiting for someone."

"Sure, go ahead," the boy nodded. "We won't be having much of a rush tonight."

He looked lonesome and bored. Ordi-narily, Jenny would have chatted with him, but she felt far too keyed up to make light conversation.

Her nervousness increased as the hands of the wall clock edged past the half hour. It was over a year since she had seen Mark. Wondering whether he had changed much during their separation, she hoped that he hadn't been too upset at her surprised reappearance. It must have been a shock to learn that she had left college and come north to track him down!

Another fifteen minutes passed. Jenny's glass was almost empty when the door opened with a whoosh of cold air and a tall, dark-haired young man entered the shop.

"Mark! I thought you'd never get here!" she cried joyfully when he carried a glass of cola over to the table and pulled out the chair opposite hers. Aware that the soda jerk was watching them, she lowered her voice. "You look so thin! But I guess I'm not used to seeing you out of uniform. Why didn't you write me? What on earth —"

"Whoa, Sis!" he protested with an amused grin.

"I'll tell you everything I can. First, though, I want to know how you traced me to the docks that day."

"It wasn't easy! Those monkeys you sent me were the only clue I had. The package was postmarked San Francisco —"

Jenny launched into a breathless account of the search through Chinatown's curio shops and of their lucky meeting with Soong Chi. "When he described the clothes you and your companions were wearing, I decided to try the waterfront," she added. "We had just about given up hope when I saw you coming down that gangplank."

"Holy mackerel!" Mark looked a bit stunned at the detective work she had undertaken. A rueful smile spread across his tanned face. "Quite the little blood-hound, aren't you? I only sent the statuette to reassure you. From your ad, I gather that you figured out its meaning."

Jenny nodded emphatically. "I knew you couldn't be involved in anything wrong — not even when the Shore Patrolmen practically accused you of being a deserter! They were only pretending to look for you, weren't they? Please tell me what this is all about."

"The S.P.'s were just following orders. But it's true; they weren't really after me," her brother confessed. "Actually, this whole scheme was the Navy's idea. We had to make it look good in case others located you to check up on me. I didn't dare write — but I couldn't stand to have you worrying too much."

"Ha! I'll be finding gray hairs any day now!" Jenny snorted. But it was a relief to know she hadn't been followed that evening outside the college library. She leaned across the table. "Mark, what's all this about the Center? I've been frantic ever since you mentioned it last night. It is a reputable organization, isn't it?"

"Sure; completely on the level," he declared. "The only black mark against them is their close association with the Marsh Shipping Lines. The Government has been keeping an eye on that outfit since the first pirate raid took place. After the Center's goods started showing up behind the Bamboo Curtain, they decided to send in an undercover man to take an even closer look at the company. Me."

"Oh! So that's why you presumably deserted the Navy!"

"Yes, they did a thorough job of blackening my name." Mark grinned. "My superiors figured that while a regular FBI or CIA agent might have trouble joining the pirate ranks, the hijackers just might decide to take on an experienced naval officer who had disgraced his uniform." His blue eyes sparkled with excitement. "And it worked!"

Jenny's face showed her consternation. She choked out a numb whisper. "You're not —"

"Not yet. It took time to make the right contacts. Finally I was approached by those two cutthroats you saw on the pier. They're old Marsh Line employees — with a profitable sideline."

"Piracy?" Jenny gulped.

"Right on the first guess. Apparently, the right kind of recruits are hard to get for that particular crew. They've been sticking to me closer than adhesive tape, assessing my evil character, no doubt. But I think I've finally convinced them that I'm a wrong 'un. They're attending a powwow with the pirate chief himself tonight. That's how I was able to get away to meet you."

He explained that naval investigators had located her through the ad and had learned that she was living with a family connected with the Center.

"I was plenty worried about you until they checked on Dr. Avery and found out what a fine reputation he has," Mark admitted.

"The Averys have been awfully kind to me," Jenny told him. "They're worried about the Center's future, though, and so am I. Isn't there any way the Navy can stop those raids?"

"That's where I come in again," Mark said grimly. "My two unsavory cohorts are nominating me for crew membership tonight. If all goes well, I'll be aboard the pirate ship next time she sails!"

# Chapter Twelve

Jenny's face turned white with horror. She had never heard of such a foolhardy plan! How could the Navy ask Mark to jeopardize his life on so wild a venture?

"Hey! Don't look so terrified," her brother pleaded. "The idea isn't nearly as dangerous as it sounds. All I have to do is let off a couple of flares to signal the ship's position to the Coast Guard. Then I dive overboard, the authorities move in, and presto! — no more pirates!"

Jenny shook her head stubbornly. "I don't like it a bit. What are the hijackers supposed to be doing while you're playing with fireworks? One tiny slip, and presto! — no more Lieutenant Mark Sheldon!"

"Pessimist! Really, Sis, I don't think anything will go wrong. Anyway, I have a duty to perform. I can't back out now."

Jenny knew that she could argue for a week and never budge him from this position. "I suppose you can't," she said in a small unhappy voice. "If only there were some way to get the evidence you need before they sail!"

"They're too cagey to risk making a move in advance," Mark grumbled. "I probably won't even meet the pirate chief until we're under way. The Navy still hasn't a clue to his identity."

"Oh!" Jenny berated herself for not having thought to mention this before. "Mark, the oddest things have been happening, practically at our own back door! Last Sunday night I saw a boat head straight in for the beach — and then vanish. And the man in the next house up the hill spends every waking moment staring at the ocean through a spyglass. He's going under the name of Briswald. But I wouldn't be surprised if that were an alias!"

Her words tumbled out in an eager stream as she told him of her encounter with the nervous woman at the mailbox. "She was in such a rush to get back to the house that she dropped a letter without noticing it," Jenny declared breathlessly. "It was addressed to the Briswalds' street number, all right — but the name on the envelope was Captain Amos Bohling!"

Mark showed a keen interest in her description of the couple's strange behavior. "It could be that you've stumbled across something important," he told her, jotting the information down in his notebook.

"Van Gilbert, Hammond Marsh's nephew, is suspicious of him, too," Jenny added. "Van believes that Mr. Briswald may be the lookout for the pirate gang. There is a fine view of the harbor from his house. He could wait for the Center's ship to put out to sea, then alert the hijackers."

"Your friend could be right," Mark acknowledged with a frown. "Although how the gang could assemble on such short notice beats me. But I'll have my superiors investigate immediately. Meanwhile, you steer clear of that fellow. Understand? On no account are you to do any more detective work."

"Don't worry! I wouldn't set foot on his property if you paid me!"

Jenny fully intended to keep her word. Unfortunately, she had no idea then how short a time her promise would last.

Soon afterward, Mark left the ice-cream parlor. There were still a hundred things Jenny wanted to discuss with him, and all sorts of questions she longed to ask. But he didn't dare remain away from San Francisco much longer. One misstep would ruin weeks of diligent planning.

"We'll have plenty of time to talk when this is over," he promised. "I know I can trust your discretion, Sis. And try not to worry, even if you don't hear from me in quite a while."

"All right. Please be careful," Jenny implored, walking partway to the door with him.

Only a few customers had entered the shop in the last hour, and no one had paid any attention to the pair talking quietly at the rear table. However, just as Mark strode out to the street a newcomer brushed past him and hurried inside.

Russ MacAllister glanced in perplexity over his shoulder, then back at Jenny. "Hi," he greeted her. "Dr. Avery told me where you were. I had dropped in to see you, and thought you might like a ride home." He cast another puzzled frown at the now empty street. "I didn't interrupt anything, did I? Who was that fellow who just left?"

"That was no fellow; that was my brother," Jenny quipped.

Instantly she clapped a hand to her lips, wishing she could recall her heedless words. What a thing to blurt out when Mark was counting on her silence!

Russ couldn't help noticing her stricken

look. "Jenny, I've never seen you so pale! Something's the matter, isn't it? Are you in any sort of trouble? Or is it your brother who needs help?" He paused, wrinkling his forehead. "It's funny; I seem to recall having seen him somewhere —"

The soda jerk was eyeing them with renewed interest, Jenny noted desperately. The last thing she wanted was to be asked any more questions — especially within earshot of an inquisitive stranger.

She grasped Russ's arm, urging him toward the door. "I'd like to go home now," she said shakily. "Please!"

"Golly, you *are* upset!" With genuine concern, Russ dashed across the sidewalk and jerked open the car door. "Quick, get in before you catch pneumonia!"

Jenny slumped against the seat cushions, glad to be out of the teeming rain, but by no means comfortable. She tried frantically to think of some subject of conversation that would decoy Russ's attention away from Mark.

He was not to be sidetracked, however. Sliding into the driver's seat, he continued to concentrate on the elusive memory. Suddenly he snapped his fingers.

"No wonder he looked familiar! His picture was splashed all over the front page a few weeks back — something about a naval officer going AWOL." Behind the horn-rimmed glasses his gray eyes widened in disbelief. "Jenny, don't tell me that deserter is your brother!"

She had to do something, say something. She and Russ were friends, but even friendship wouldn't prevent an honest citizen from reporting a wanted man to the police!

"I didn't tell you. You guessed," she groaned, able to think of no fabrication to substitute for the truth. "And he's not a deserter!"

"But the newspapers —"

"There was a reason for those misleading headlines." Jenny gazed earnestly at him, trying to read the thoughts behind his worried expression. "Russ, can I trust you? Really trust you? Because if not, what I'm going to tell you may cost my brother his life."

"That sounds pretty serious," he said quietly. "You don't have to break any confidences for my sake, Jenny. Just let me know that everything is all right, and I'll take you home. You have my word that I'll never mention this to anyone."

She blinked rapidly, squeezing back the tears that threatened to spill down her cheeks. A ghost of a smile brightened her wan features.

"Thanks. That pledge of allegiance did a lot to bolster my morale. Mark told me he'd trust my discretion. Since you've learned this much, it would probably be best if I told you the whole story."

Positive that her faith in Russ would not be betrayed, she detailed the bewildering experiences of the last month.

"Now you know why I was so afraid someone was following me, that day your car kept popping up behind us on the road. And you can see how vital it is that Mark's coming here tonight be kept secret," she finished. "He took a terrible risk just to reassure me. I could have bitten my tongue when I blurted out his real identity to you!"

Russ could only shake his head in admiration. "You Sheldons certainly have courage!" he exclaimed. "Mark sounds like the sort of man who could carry out any perilous assignment successfully. And not all sisters would have gone on trusting him as you did, either, in spite of all the evidence against him."

Unconsciously, Jenny straightened her shoulders. It had been a tremendous relief to confide her doubts and fears to Russ.

She had dated many boys during her years in high school and college, but never anyone so understanding and easy to talk to as Russ.

"Even so, it's been a strain," she admitted. "I'll be glad when it's all over!"

But the tense period of waiting wouldn't end until August, Jenny reminded herself glumly later that night. It was strange to find her emotions regarding that fateful period being stretched in two directions. With half her mind, she wished that the date would come quickly so that Mark's dangerous undertaking could soon be finished. Yet, too, she longed to have the summer days that she shared with Russ linger on and on.

Russ would sail on the same ship that her brother was risking his life to protect. Monterey without him would be a different, lonely place. She was going to find it hard to say good-bye.

With difficulty, Jenny wrenched her thoughts away from the sandy-haired young man who had won her enduring affection, and concentrated on a more immediate problem. The Averys. Should she tell them about Mark's visit?

After much pondering, she decided

against doing so. It wasn't mistrust that kept her silent. She felt positive that neither the professor nor Miss Ursula would intentionally reveal the Navy's daring plan. But a slip of the tongue could be made by anyone.

With a twinge of apprehension, she remembered that the identity of the pirate chief still remained a mystery. It was just barely possible that the ringleader was in some way connected with the Center. And one unguarded word from Dr. Avery in a moment of absentmindedness —

"Discretion," Jenny murmured, settling down beneath the warm quilts, while outside, wind and rain churned the ocean into a frenzied cauldron of crashing surf. "Discretion!"

The house was damp and chilly and the kitchen deserted when Jenny came downstairs the next morning. Shivering, she pushed up the thermostat, then turned to the window for a survey of the weather.

The sun still cowered behind dingy gray clouds, but the force of the wind had abated during the night. The worst of the freak storm seemed to have passed.

Hearing footsteps above her head, Jenny hurried over to the stove. By the time Dr. Avery and Paul entered the kitchen, she had sausages sizzling and blueberry muffins toasting to a golden brown in the oven.

"Oh, boy. I smell something good!" Paul cried.

Jenny ruffled the little boy's hair and peered past him inquiringly. "Is Miss Ursula still asleep?"

Dr. Avery, looking tired and upset, shook his head. "I'm afraid she had a very bad night," he declared. "Wet weather always seems to make her arthritis much worse. I insisted that she stay in bed until the doctor arrives."

"I'm sorry to hear she isn't feeling well." Jenny inspected Paul's hands, then passed him the silverware to set on the table. "You two sit down and have your breakfast. I'll go see if I can tempt her appetite with some of these muffins."

It was plain that the crippling ailment had caused Miss Ursula a great deal of pain. Lines of suffering were etched on her sweet face, and she needed Jenny's help to sit up in bed. But she managed an uncomplaining smile at the sight of the daintily arranged tray the girl had brought upstairs with her.

"Breakfast in bed? You're treating me like a queen! I'm sorry to put you to so much trouble, my dear. Clement knows that as soon as the sun comes out, these silly old bones of mine will be back on their good behavior. By noon, I promise to be up and creaking around again."

Jenny smothered a smile at Miss Ursula's choice of words. She injected a firm note into her voice.

"You'll be up when the doctor gives his permission, and not a moment sooner! Please eat your breakfast while it's still hot."

After having pronounced the meal delicious to the last crumb, Miss Ursula lay back on her pillows. Jenny set the tray aside and smoothed the sheets. When she had made the elderly lady comfortable, she solemnly pressed a small curved object into Miss Ursula's hand.

"I know a bell would be much more dignified. But if you need anything, just give a toot on this whistle of Paul's. It's shrill enough to be heard all over the house!"

Returning to the lower floor, she found Dr. Avery hanging up the telephone. "The Wynnes recommended their personal physician, but Dr. Hogarth won't be able to come until later this morning," he said. "You two go on to church without me. I'll stay here in case I can do anything for my sister."

All through Mass, Paul behaved angelically. It wasn't often that he managed to sit still for a whole hour, and as they emerged from the crowded church Jenny glanced down at him with a look of puzzled anxiety.

"You're not coming down with a cold or the flu, are you?"

His freshly scrubbed face wore an expression of absolute innocence. "Oh, no. I feel fine. Grandpa's always telling me not to wiggle around in church, so I didn't," he added virtuously.

"Good for you! I'm fresh out of merit badges, worse luck. Will you settle for an ice-cream cone? We can run down for it after lunch."

The secret, impish merriment that Paul had kept concealed behind his bright brown eyes faded into startled disappointment. "After lunch?" he gulped. "Then — aren't you going sailing this afternoon?"

"Heavens, I forgot all about that!" The timely reminder spurred Jenny into prompt action and kept her from noticing his odd reaction to the offer of a treat. She pressed down hard on the accelerator, urging the old car up the hill as fast as the speed limit would permit.

Sorry now that she had agreed to a second cruise aboard the *Hurricane Edna*, she resolved to call Van at once. Jenny recalled how devoted he was to his invalid uncle. Surely, once she had explained that she was badly needed at home, he would understand her reasons for breaking their date.

But a search through the pages of the directory showed no number listed for either Hammond Marsh or Van Gilbert. Probably, she guessed, like many wealthy people, they preferred to keep their telephone unlisted.

Dr. Avery might know the Marsh's number, she thought. Jenny hurried out to the hall, then paused and turned back at the sound of quiet voices upstairs. This was no time to bother him with trivialities, not with Miss Ursula feeling so unwell and Dr. Hogarth already in attendance.

She would just have to meet Van on the beach and make her excuses in person.

With an eye on the clock, Jenny straightened up the downstairs rooms and prepared a hasty lunch for Paul. Regretfully, she decided that her own meal would have to wait until her return, but she covered a plate of sandwiches with a napkin and left it on the counter for the professor.

The hands of her watch pointed to one o'clock exactly when she hurried through the garden and across the crescent of sand to the water's edge. Peering expectantly down the coastline, Jenny felt a stab of chagrin. Seagulls soaring gracefully overhead and the rustle of waves lapping at the shore were her only company. Nowhere on the horizon could she distinguish a billowing white sail.

She waited an impatient few minutes, glad that she had exchanged her high heels for more practical shoes before setting out. Then, hopeful that she might be able to catch a glimpse of the Marsh's beach from a more seaward vantage point, she scrambled up onto the massive black boulders that extended a dozen or more yards out from the shoreline.

Gaining a precarious foothold on the slimy, pitted surface, Jenny shaded her eyes and strained for a sight of the *Hurricane Edna*.

What could be keeping Van?

The climb, though exhilarating, had netted her little. Unfortunately, the bulging cliffside jutting out between the Briswalds' boundary and the beginning of the Marsh property still obscured her view.

Frowning, she studied the uneven coastline. A few feet past the Briswalds' far fence the rugged hill protruded almost to the rim of the sea. At high tide only a narrow path of sand separated the base of the cliff from the whitecapped ocean surface. Beyond this, the shoreline appeared to veer sharply in again, since the greater part of the Marsh frontage was concealed from where she stood.

Jenny sighed in annoyance and glared again at her watch. Twenty past one. She was beginning to wonder whether Van's invitation to her had slipped his mind. He had seemed so steady and reliable. But it wasn't really fair to judge. Perhaps he too was needed at home and had been too rushed to call and cancel their date.

Whatever the explanation, Jenny decided to give the vigil only ten minutes more. Already she was growing chilly from the fresh ocean breeze, and her skirt was splattered with flecks of icy spray.

She picked her way carefully back along the craggy surface of the boulders and jumped down onto the sand. As she straightened up, a streak of movement farther up the beach caught her eye.

Perplexed, Jenny watched Paul cut diagonally across the sand. With the manner of someone bent on an important errand, he marched directly up to the Briswalds' fence.

In a flash, she forgot about Van's unexplained absence and concentrated on the activities of her small friend.

He has been acting awfully mysterious lately, she thought uneasily. I wonder what mischief that little dickens is up to now?

At that instant, Paul darted a wary glance at the empty garden, then shinnied nimbly up on top of the fence.

Jenny gasped in sudden alarm and flew toward him as he teetered dizzily on the high rail. She bit back the warning shout that leaped to her lips. He would fall if she startled him!

But, as it turned out, this precaution came too late. Swaying to keep his balance, Paul chanced to look in her direction. His little mouth formed a round "O" of surprise.

"Be careful!"

Jenny leaped for him, but the distance between them was still too great. Paul's foot slipped off the rough board. With his arms windmilling wildly, he somersaulted in the air. Before the echoes of her scream died away, he had landed with a bone-bruising thud on the other side of the fence.

Kicking off her shoes, Jenny splashed into the water. A precious two minutes were spent rounding the ugly "no trespassing" barrier which stretched into the sea. Half swimming, half wading, she struggled around it and tore across the low-tide mark where Paul had fallen.

His small defenseless form lay ominously still. Jenny dropped to her knees beside him. Her own breathing paused, suspended, as she frantically tested his wrist for a pulsebeat. At last, her probing fingers located a faint, flickering throb.

"Oh, thank God! He's still alive!"

Jenny stared helplessly down at him as she breathed the prayer of thanksgiving. But Paul's skin was chalk white, his limp body completely motionless. He could be dying!

It might prove fatal if she lifted him and tried to carry him home. Yet she couldn't leave him here alone, either —

So intent was Jenny on her churning thoughts that she didn't even notice the footsteps that crunched across the sand and halted directly behind her. Suddenly a gnarled hand fell on her shoulder.

Jenny's head jerked up. Her eyes, already

filled with anxiety, widened in terror.

Frowning sternly down at her was the man she suspected of being the lookout for a desperate gang of criminals. The man whom, previously, she had only glimpsed behind a spyglass.

Mr. Briswald!

# Chapter Thirteen

Jenny fought to conceal a shudder. Practically anyone else in the entire world would have been a more welcome sight than Mr. Briswald. But he was, after all, another human being. At that moment she didn't care how much skulduggery he was mixed up in!

"Oh, please, can you help me?" she implored. "He fell, and I'm so afraid —"

"Aye, I saw it happen. Move aside, miss, while I have a look at the lad."

No one would have dared disobey that gruff, commanding voice. Jenny stepped back and watched fearfully while Mr. Briswald examined Paul's inert body for broken bones. His massive hands moved deftly and with a surprising gentleness over the boy's arms and legs.

"No fractures," he reported shortly. "Perhaps a slight concussion. Shock and exposure are the biggest dangers. He'll be better off inside."

"You mean, up — there?"

Jenny quailed inwardly as she stared at

the bleak exterior of the hillside house. But she was given no chance to protest. Effortlessly, Mr. Briswald hoisted Paul in his arms and strode across the sand to a winding gravel pathway.

Struggling to keep up with his rapid gait, Jenny limped stocking-footed along behind them. Over to one side she caught a glimpse of a well-tended vegetable garden. The otherwise neglected slope boasted no flowers, no outdoor furniture — nothing that a householder might want to protect from careless picnickers.

Again she wondered at the reason for the fence. Why were the Briswalds so determined to shut out the rest of the world? And having obtained such an elaborate amount of privacy, why was their taciturn neighbor now allowing her and Paul to enter his stronghold?

She quickened her pace to walk protectively alongside the unconscious boy. It was too late now to prevent him from being taken inside. But she intended to make sure that he remained there no longer than absolutely necessary.

Mr. Briswald paused at the back entrance and nudged the door open with one of his burly shoulders. Not until Jenny had followed him across the threshold and stepped onto the spotlessly waxed surface of the kitchen floor did she give a thought to her own bedraggled appearance.

A dozen runs crisscrossed her nylons, torn from stumbling up the gravel path. Sand and water weighed down her skirt, causing the sodden material to cling grittily to her skin, while stains from the briny sea water ridged her blouse. No wonder Mrs. Briswald eyed her in such consternation when she shuffled, dripping, across that shining linoleum!

But after one open-mouthed glance at Jenny, Martha Briswald transferred her attention to the small bundle in her husband's arms.

"Oh, the poor wee lamb!" she cried. "Amos, what happened to him? He's not — ?"

"The lad's come to no serious harm. Get some blankets, woman!"

Cowed by his stern manner, Mrs. Briswald hurried from the room. During her absence her husband carefully lowered Paul to the chintz-covered sofa that stood to one side of the enormous kitchen range. A moment later, the boy was being swathed from toe to chin in downy-soft coverlets.

Bending anxiously over him, Jenny

noticed that his breathing had become deeper and more regular now. She brushed a straw-colored lock back from his forehead, and rose, facing the Briswalds.

"May I use your telephone, please?" she asked. "Dr. Avery should be notified at once. I know he will want his grandson to have prompt medical attention."

The gray-haired couple looked uneasily at one another. For a time, Jenny feared that her request would be refused. Then, almost defiantly, Mrs. Briswald nodded and pointed to the adjoining room.

"Go ahead. The telephone is in there."

Jenny spun quickly around and almost ran through the doorway, afraid that Mr. Briswald might countermand his wife's decision. Hurrying across the hooked rug to the maple end table on which the phone stood, she could hear their voices raised in sharp debate.

Half a minute later, she was describing Paul's accident to Dr. Avery. There was no chance to prepare him for the bad news, and his voice quavered with shock when he replied.

"Thank goodness Dr. Hogarth hasn't left yet! The next house up the hill, you say? Stay with him, Jenny. We'll be right there!"

The line went dead in her ear. In relief, Jenny replaced the receiver. She had done all she could for Paul. Anything more would be up to the doctor.

With the burden of responsibility lifted from her shoulders, she was able to relax somewhat. She couldn't resist pausing for a moment to gaze around the living room.

This part of the house, too, was scrupulously tidy. Not a speck of dust marred any of the tabletops, and even the portraits on the walls glowed softly with a dull sheen of polish. Jenny noticed with interest that the men who had been immortalized on canvas bore an austere resemblance to one another — and to her reluctant host. Although the style of clothes had changed from generation to generation, they were all unmistakably attired in the garb of sea captains.

Apparently, following the sea was a tradition in the Briswald family. Jenny wondered if the model ships, painstakingly built into bottles that graced the mantel, were replicas of the vessels those long-dead mariners had commanded.

It wasn't until she had started back toward the door that she spotted the most intriguing picture of all. Rather than another oil painting, this was the fairly recent photograph of a merchant ship. The name *Yankee Trader* was lettered on her bow.

A familiar face leaped out at Jenny from among the crewmen standing on the dock alongside the ship. Mr. Briswald, looking almost youthful, smiled out from the center of the group. From the uniform he wore, she guessed that he had been the vessel's master.

Jenny was both fascinated and puzzled by this glimpse into the man's background. Mr. Briswald was not much over fifty, she judged. Sea captains rarely retired so young. She wondered what had caused him to break with family tradition and abandon the maritime service.

Intent on these speculations, she had paid no attention to the voices droning on in the adjacent room. But suddenly Mrs. Briswald's tone rose in agitation.

"I told you no good would come of that fence. See what's happened now!"

"The boy had no business trying to climb over it," her husband growled. "It was built to keep people away. I cannot abide folks coming around to stare at us!"

"Why should they bother? No one here knows who you are — or cares!" came the distressed reply. "Amos, what good does it do to keep on living in the past? How I wish we had never come here —"

Sobs muffled the rest of her words. Embarrassed, Jenny drew back from the doorway. Perhaps, she thought, the key to Mr. Briswald's mysterious behavior lay in a tragic past, and not in some up-to-date wrongdoing. Although her suspicions of the man had not been entirely allayed, she couldn't bring herself to eavesdrop any longer.

A minute later, she cleared her throat warningly before entering the kitchen. She addressed Mr. Briswald and studiously ignored his wife's anguished expression.

"Paul's grandfather and Dr. Hogarth will be here soon. Has there been any change in his condition yet?"

"I believe he will regain consciousness before long." The former sea captain narrowed a calculating look at her. "Why was the boy trying to trespass on my property?"

Jenny returned his gaze levelly. "I don't know, Mr. Briswald. But I am positive that it was not with the intention of damaging anything."

To mask the worry in her eyes, she stared down at the small figure on the couch. Why *had* Paul risked climbing over that fence? A disconcerting idea popped into her mind. The day he had gone for that forbidden swim, Paul had been trying to tell her something — something about a "bad man." But what? She blamed herself now for not having paid closer attention. If only she could remember!

Just then, however, a stifled groan escaped the boy's lips. Jenny's heart fluttered with joy as Paul's eyes blinked open.

"He's coming to!"

Her elation waned, though, when he continued to regard her with a blank stare.

"Paul? Honey, don't you know me? You've been hurt, but you'll be better very soon," she whispered, trying to ease his look of pained bewilderment.

Her words were interrupted by the chiming of the doorbell. A moment afterward, Mrs. Briswald ushered Dr. Avery into the kitchen. He was followed by a short, competent-looking man carrying a black bag.

After making a thorough examination, Dr. Hogarth assured them that there was no cause for alarm.

"A few days' bed rest, and this young chap will be as active as ever," he declared. "Don't worry if some of his recollections are a bit hazy at first. A severe bump on the head occasionally results in a case of temporary amnesia, but this soon clears up."

Weak-kneed with relief, Jenny gripped Dr. Avery's arm. Deep creases lined the professor's face, and she worried that the strain might prove too much for him. Nevertheless, he managed to thank the Briswalds for the care they had given Paul.

"Right now I can think of nothing except getting my grandson safely home," he added tremulously. "But someday I will try to repay you for your kindness."

Mr. Briswald shrugged his gratitude aside. "Anyone would have done the same. You owe us nothing."

He remained stubbornly in the kitchen while his wife escorted the party to the front door. Jenny lagged behind for a moment when the men carried Paul out to the car. Her pity had been aroused by this gaunt, unhappy woman with the careworn face.

"I wish you'd come visit us soon. You'd like Miss Ursula, I know," she suggested shyly. "She is lonesome, too, up here away from all her friends."

From the woman's wistful expression, Jenny knew that she longed to accept the offer of friendship. But something, probably fear of her husband's reaction, made Mrs. Briswald shake her head.

Who wouldn't look careworn, Jenny thought, if he had to live with a dour old curmudgeon like Amos Briswald? She had no time to brood over her neighbor's sad life, however. Paul was still too befuddled to do much for himself. With the doctor's help, she got him tucked into bed. When he was sleeping quietly, she urged the professor to stretch out for a rest also.

"Take the young lady's advice. I doubt that she could cope with three invalids." Dr. Hogarth supported her suggestion.

On the way out, he assured her that he would drop by again in the morning. "Miss Avery should be up and around by then," he added. "Her arthritis is painful, but not especially severe. I'll consider you a wonderful nurse if you can keep them all from worrying about each other."

As soon as the door had closed behind him, Jenny collapsed wearily into a chair. She found it hard to believe that it was only mid-afternoon. So much had happened already that day!

She closed her eyes, then wrenched them open again as the phone shrilled. Now what?

"Will you accept my apology?" Van's

penitent voice said in her ear. "The *Hurricane Edna*'s mast snapped just as I was taking her out. By the time I had finished making repairs, one o'clock was long gone."

"That's all right. I couldn't have gone sailing today anyway." Jenny explained about Miss Ursula's illness, and added that Paul had suffered an accident. "This place is beginning to resemble a field hospital!"

"Then there's no chance of your having dinner with me tonight?"

"I'm afraid not, Van. They need me here."

She hung up with a trace of irritation. Van wasn't the only one with a sense of responsibility. Had he really expected her to desert a sick family for the sake of a last-minute dinner date?

It occurred to Jenny that had her caller been Russ, he would probably have offered to come over and help with the dishes. A pensive smile crossed her face. There was a great deal of difference between the two young men. She enjoyed Van's company, and he was undoubtedly better looking than Russ. But as for thoughtfulness, he couldn't begin to compare!

Then her conscience prickled with remorse. She was reading too much into a casual invitation. After all, didn't Van accompany his uncle everywhere? That was real devotion!

Or just plain common sense!

A new thought struck her, and she giggled a little at the mental argument she seemed to be having with herself. It didn't matter to her, one way or another, nor was it any of her business. But Dr. Avery had mentioned that Van was Hammond Marsh's only living relative. And Mr. Marsh was a very rich man.

Some nephews might be kind to wealthy, aged uncles in hopes of someday inheriting a fortune.

Brilliant sunshine awoke Jenny on Monday morning. The last vestiges of the storm were gone, and the warm, dry weather in the days following did a great deal to restore Miss Ursula to health.

In spite of the doctor's optimism, however, Jenny continued to worry about Paul. Apparently, the temporary amnesia brought on by his fall affected only the events of the past few days. He remembered everyone's names and quickly recovered his mischievous good spirits. But he was genuinely astonished when she told him that he had fallen from the fence.

"Gosh, did I really do a dumb thing like that?" he asked, unable to recall why he had risked the climb.

"Yes. Remember promising me that you wouldn't go swimming alone again? You probably intended to stay on dry land but still go farther down the beach. Climbing the fence was the only way to accomplish that. Can't you think of any reason why you took such a chance?"

"I don't know, Jenny. Honest!"

It was useless to ask him any more questions. She sighed and patted his hand to convince him that it didn't really matter. In time, Paul's memory might return. If it didn't —

Jenny frowned, wondering why it suddenly seemed so important that she learn the identity of the "bad man" and why Paul had been chased by him. That day on the beach she had just assumed that her little friend was referring to Mr. Briswald. Now she wasn't quite so sure.

"He could have been talking about anyone," she mulled aloud. "I don't suppose the incident had any real significance. Still — I'd like to know."

It was still necessary for Miss Ursula to take frequent rests, and with Paul under doctor's orders to remain in bed, Jenny was kept too busy even to step out of doors during the few days following his accident. Russ commented disapprovingly on her pallor when he stopped by for a visit on Wednesday evening.

"Get your sweater and I'll take you for a walk. Even Florence Nightingale must have taken a fresh-air break once in a while," he declared.

Delighted at seeing him again, Jenny suggested that they stroll down by the beach.

"I feel terrible about not following through on the book-collection plan," she apologized. "Next week we should be back to normal here. I'll have more time to work on the project then."

"You're working too hard already. As a matter of fact, your ads have stimulated quite a response. For days now, all sorts of people have been drifting into the Center to add two or three books apiece to our traveling library. It's amazing how eager everyone is to help," Russ told her enthusiastically.

"I'm glad. You won't mind having to cope with the extra baggage, will you?"

Jenny leaned against the garden gate. A sweet scent of jasmine perfumed the moonlit air, and she knew that all her life the aroma of that flower would remind her of Russ. "It's strange to think that in a few short weeks you will be living in a different world, far away from here."

"Yes. I can't quite imagine what it will be like" His arm rested lightly on her shoulders. He looked earnest, and rather sad.

"Up until a month or two ago, this trip was the most important goal in my life," he said quietly. "I didn't think any girl would ever make me want to change my mind. But you have, Jenny. Two years away from you is going to seem like an eternity."

He leaned forward, and for an instant his lips rested gently on hers. To Jenny's soaring heart, the moment was like an old-fashioned Fourth of July, with Roman candles and bombs bursting in air.

A second splintering report shattered the magic spell. It was an unromantic letdown to discover that the sounds which had exploded during their kiss were not sky-rockets but hammer blows.

"What the dickens?" Russ stepped back, staring in annoyance at the shoreline.

Jenny eased open the gate latch and drew him down the steps to the sand. "It's coming from over there. Oh, Russ, look — that's Mr. Briswald. He's tearing down his fence!"

"The gimlet-eyed spyglass-watcher? I thought you said he had an obsession about privacy."

"He does — or did. But his wife, poor woman, doesn't agree. Maybe she persuaded him to take it down because of what happened to Paul."

Russ twined his fingers protectively around her hand, and for several minutes they stood in the shadow of the terrace wall watching Amos Briswald toil to uproot his fence.

"You know, I believe I was wrong about him," Jenny whispered at last. "He's cranky and standoffish as can be, but there's sort of a rock-ribbed honesty about him, too. He must have a valid reason for shunning the rest of the world. Somehow, after meeting him, I can't quite visualize him as a spy for a gang of pirates."

Russ guided her back to the house. "Don't be too trusting. Since your brother isn't around to take care of you, I intend to. As long as I can, anyway," he added glumly. "You don't know how much I wish —"

The back door opened abruptly, and Dr. Avery peered out at them. "Oh, there you are, Jenny," he said. "You are wanted on the telephone."

"First hammers, now bells," Russ grumbled. "Never mind. I'll be back tomorrow — with my books."

There was nothing Jenny could do but say good night and hurry inside. Still wondering what it was Russ had intended to tell her before the interruption, she glared disgustedly at the receiver.

The sound of Mark's voice, however, swiftly dispelled her resentment.

"Jenny?" he said in a low cautious tone. "The Navy has run a quick check on that neighbor you were telling me about. It seems your suspicions were well founded. There is something definitely fishy about Amos Bohling — alias Mr. Briswald!"

# Chapter Fourteen

"Fishy?" Jenny repeated. His words came as a shock, especially since she had almost succeeded in persuading herself that Mr. Briswald was only a harmless eccentric. "Then his name really is Amos Bohling?"

"Yes, and he has enough of the necessary qualifications to convince my superiors that he may actually be our elusive pirate chief!" Mark's voice quickened with excitement. "I've only time to hit the high points of the story," he went on, "but until just about a year ago Bohling was the highly respected skipper of the *Yankee Trader*, a merchant vessel operating on the East Coast. One stormy night his ship collided with another craft. Both steamers sank as a result of the crash."

"How dreadful!" Jenny could almost picture the panic that must have ensued as lifeboats were hastily lowered onto the pitch-black ocean. "Who was blamed for the catastrophe?"

"One guess. The helmsman of the *Yankee Trader* had suddenly been taken ill, and Captain Bohling took over the wheel himself that night. He was the only person on the bridge at the time of the collision," Mark told her. "On the other hand, several officers from the *Nantucket* were in a position to see what happened. They testified later that the *Yankee Trader* cut directly in front of their ship.

"Captain Bohling told a different version of the crash, but he had no witnesses to help him prove his innocence. At the trial, the word of the *Nantucket*'s crew was believed. In spite of his excellent record, and the bravery he showed towing four of his injured crewmen to safety, the Maritime Board cited Bohling for negligence and relieved him of his command."

"That would be enough to embitter anyone," Jenny said. "I wonder, though, if even that would make an honest man turn to piracy. Mark, is there something else you haven't told me?"

"Not much. Just that the *Nantucket* was owned by the Marsh Shipping Lines!"

"Oh, good heavens! He certainly must bear a grudge against that company."

"Exactly," Mark affirmed. "Can you think of a better way than hijacking to revenge himself on the outfit that ruined him?"

"I can't, no." Jenny wondered what her brother would say if he learned that only a few days ago she had spent over an hour in the suspected man's house. She decided that there was no point in telling him.

"Will this new information have any effect on your mission?" she asked instead.

"Probably not. Suspecting the man of piracy is one thing; proving it will be something else again," he reminded her. "He and his crew will have to be caught red-handed. And I'm afraid there is still only one way to do that."

"Darn! I was hoping — Mark, please don't take any unnecessary chances," Jenny implored. "I worry dreadfully about your being mixed up with that band of cut-throats."

"We settled all that last time, remember, Sis?" Mark's voice dropped lower. "Have to go now. I'll be in touch — if and when I can."

Jenny turned away from the phone feeling thoroughly confused and a little disheartened. Obviously, Mark and his superiors felt that they had found the right man. Mr. Briswald — no, Captain Bohling, she corrected herself — certainly had an ideal motive for vengeance against the Marsh Line.

But why should he choose to attack only those ships that had been lent to the Center? Puzzled, Jenny trudged slowly upstairs. It didn't make sense.

Even with the door to her balcony closed against the night air, she could still hear the echoing thud of hammer blows against the fence. An icy finger of apprehension snaked up her spine. Supposing the lead she had given Mark proved to be false? If the Navy concentrated its attention on the wrong man, her brother might be in greater danger than ever!

True to his promise, Russ brought his language hooks up to the house the next night. Dr. Avery sat in on the study session to help with their pronunciation, so Jenny wasn't able to tell him then of the information the naval inspectors had uncovered.

But on Saturday Miss Ursula shooed Jenny out of the house, insisting that the invalids had been pampered long enough. With time now on her hands, Jenny invited Russ to accompany her on a round of the libraries located in nearby towns.

"You can see why I'm perturbed," she confided during the short scenic drive to Pacific Grove. "What if Mr. Briswald-Bohling isn't involved at all? The real

197

pirates may be able to hold up your ship if the Coast Guard is keeping tabs on the wrong suspect!"

Russ tried to reassure her. "Look at it another way. There's a good chance he will turn out to be 'it.' If you hadn't told them about your weird neighbor, no one might ever have connected him with the hijackings." He glowered at her in mock despair. "For Pete's sake, quit stewing about it, Jenny. Didn't Mark promise you that nothing would go wrong?"

She couldn't help smiling at this expression of blind faith. "He did at that. Maybe I should carry around my little statuette of the monkeys, to serve as a reminder!"

Books, books, and more books!

In the weeks that followed, Jenny spent four or five afternoons a week at the Center, cataloguing, sorting, and crating the volumes that continued to flow in. The donations included many of the items Dr. Wynne had hoped to receive — books for children, practical self-help volumes, and even a few foreign language translations.

One day early in August, Elaine Kendall bustled into the temporary library that Jenny had set up. She looked carefully over the titles that had been set aside for shipment to Bengali.

"What a help these are going to be!" she exclaimed. "I've been so tied up with earning my degree that I haven't thought of anything but medicine for months. Medicine and Walt," the lovely blonde girl added with a radiant smile. "He writes that the epidemic is under control at last. Maybe if he and Nate and I can keep the natives healthy, they'll be more interested in learning a few things about the outside world."

"Nate will be posted in Bengali too?" Jenny asked. "Yes, and we're so lucky to have him. He's a first-rate diagnostician, even though he does look like a football player."

After Elaine had continued onto the lab, Jenny slipped an encyclopedia of sports in with the other volumes earmarked for Bengali. Dr. Nate Benedict might wind up coaching a jungle Little League!

All through the summer the former warehouse now occupied by the Center had resounded to the activity of construction work taking place in the east wing. Passing through that part of the building later in the same week, Jenny was astonished to see how much progress had been made toward the completion of Dr.

Wynne's long-dreamed-of clinic.

She commented on this to the director next time she saw him.

"By the end of the year our training program ought to be well launched," he said proudly. "Already a dedicated young doctor from India has arrived to approve the plans we are making to instruct some of his countrymen. Dr. Ramanathan's wife is currently undergoing some delicate heart surgery up at Stanford Hospital. Because of this, his small daughter has also accompanied him to America. Perhaps you could help entertain her during some of our conferences."

"I'd enjoy doing so," Jenny said.

"Unfortunately, the child knows only a few words of English," Dr. Wynne warned. "Could you come in tomorrow morning at nine?"

She hesitated only a moment before agreeing. Since his accident, Paul had shown no inclination to rove further than their own back garden. Troubled by the blank spot in his memory, he seemed almost afraid to venture close to the beach alone. Remembering this, Jenny felt that Miss Ursula would have no difficulty in looking after him by herself. She therefore had no reluctance in offering to spend a few extra hours at the Center.

Her heart was immediately captivated by Nadjia Ramanathan's huge brown eyes and shy, appealing manner. The dainty little Indian girl was attired in a miniature sari. Jenny began trying to make friends by admiring the beautiful dress, but although Nadjia listened politely, it soon became clear that the child didn't understand what she was saying.

"Oh, my. Let's see if I know enough Hindi, then."

Haltingly, Jenny rephrased her sentence. At once Nadjia's face brightened, and she responded with a torrent of words.

Jenny laughed, holding up a hand in protest. "Slower! I am just learning!"

Nadjia made a game of their language difficulties. Pointing to various objects in the room, she pronounced their names in Hindi. Jenny repeated the words after her, then translated them into English for the child to say.

Before long, they had become firm friends. They were still giggling over each other's accents when Deedee Jay strolled down the hall and paused in the doorway.

"What's all the hilarity? If you've learned a new joke, tell me, too."

"We're forming a class. Sort of a

kindergarten," Jenny told her when she had managed to stop laughing. "Come join us. Practice your Hindi on Nadjia. In the past hour I've developed a whole new vocabulary."

Deedee was only too pleased at the chance to demonstrate her fluency in the foreign tongue. The time passed unnoticed while they took turns making up funny sentences for Nadjia to correct. None of the girls noticed that the door to the adjoining room had opened until Dr. Wynne stepped over the threshold.

"Well, you sound very happy in here," he observed. "You do your teacher credit, Mrs. Jay. But I'm sure I heard a third voice speaking Hindi. Was that you, Jenny?"

She nodded, embarrassed at learning that their silly conversation had filtered through the walls of his office.

"Yes, I learned a few words of the language from helping Russ MacAllister with his homework. I'm sorry if we disturbed your conference."

He waved aside the apology and gazed at her appraisingly. "It seems that the Center has overlooked a fine potential volunteer. We could use many more workers to help with our program in India. Doesn't the thought of that sort of life appeal to you?"

"Oh, it does!" Jenny exclaimed. "I'd volunteer in a minute if I were able to do anything useful. But I've only had library training, not medical experience like Elaine and Deedee."

"Disease and lack of food are not the only problems confronting these underdeveloped nations," he declared. "Ignorance is another great handicap. People must learn something of what goes on outside their own villages before they can become good citizens. A person who knows and loves books could assist even the most backward community along the road to progress."

He looked at his watch. "I have an appointment, or I would stay and try to persuade you that the Center needs your help in the field. But it is too late to think of having you join the current group of volunteers, since they will be sailing for the Orient within a few days. We will talk more about this another time."

Before he left to take Nadjia back to her father, he asked if Jenny would mind spending one more morning taking care of the child.

"Of course not. I'll gladly come back again tomorrow," Jenny murmured.

Her mind was awhirl with the possibilities Dr. Wynne had suggested. If only she had discussed this with him in June, she might be sailing on the same ship with Russ and Deedee and Bruce!

Then she remembered Mark, and her daydreams burst. She couldn't possibly make any plans for the future until he was no longer in danger.

Nadjia had some exciting news to tell Jenny the next day. Speaking very slowly so that the older girl would be sure to understand, she bubbled that her mother's operation had been a complete success. Before long, the Ramanathan family would be returning to India.

"That's wonderful, honey." Jenny smiled back at her. "Some of my friends are going to visit your country soon, too. Would you like to help me pack the rest of these books for them to take along?"

She was careful to speak quietly, remembering how yesterday their gay conversation had penetrated the thin wall partitions. It wouldn't do to disturb the director two days in a row!

By mid-morning, they had nearly completed the chore. As a special treat, Jenny took Nadjia out to the soft-drink machine in the reception room and filled two cups with ice-cold cola for them to sip while they worked. They had just reentered the makeshift library when she heard the trundle of wheels outside in the corridor, followed by a tap at the adjoining door.

"Why, Mr. Marsh!" Dr. Wynne genially greeted his visitor. "What a pleasant surprise. Come in, come in."

There was a bump as the wheelchair rolled over the threshold. "You can run along now, Van. I won't be needing you for a while," Hammond Marsh grunted.

Jenny paused in the act of knotting a cord around one of the cumbersome crates, hoping that Van Gilbert would not pass the library and catch a glimpse of her. On several occasions during the past few weeks he had called to ask her out, but each time she had refused, preferring to spend the time with Russ. It might be a trifle awkward having to face him now.

Luckily, his footsteps faded away in the opposite direction. With Nadjia's eager assistance, Jenny continued with the task of tying and labeling the boxes of books. As busy as she was, though, she could not avoid overhearing much of the conversation that took place next door.

"I take it you have been touring our new clinic," Dr. Wynne said. "The construction is coming along at a fine rate, don't you agree?"

Mr. Marsh's voice sounded a trifle querulous. "Yes, yes, I suppose so. But frankly, Dr. Wynne, I made this trip down here today for another purpose. I want to know if you've found out any more about these bandits who are attacking my ships."

"Everything possible has been done to try to apprehend them. The authorities are working on the problem, too." The director tried to placate him. "It's a shame —"

"Shame! It's an outrage, that's what it is! And I'm still not convinced that this — this piracy isn't being masterminded by someone right here at the Center!"

"No one here would do such a terrible thing," Derek Wynne said in defense of his staff. "What possible reason could they have?"

"I don't know," Hammond Marsh snapped. "But if those marauders touch one more of my ships, it will mean the end of our association. The Center will never get another nickel out of me!"

Jenny sat shock-still as the echoes of this angry ultimatum died away. For a moment there was silence in the director's office, too. Fervently wishing that she and Nadjia had stayed in the reception room to drink their Cokes, she started to say something reassuring to the startled child.

She opened her mouth to speak, then paused, the words frozen on her lips. From outside in the hall she had caught the whisper of a stealthy footstep.

Someone besides herself had been listening to the irate discussion. Someone who might have no business being in the Center at all, let alone eavesdropping on an argument best kept private!

# Chapter Fifteen

Jenny poised in a crouch, scarcely daring to breathe. Nadjia, too, sat like a small round-eyed statue. No further sound betrayed the listener in the hall. Had he gone? wondered Jenny. Or was he still hovering nearby, with his ear pressed close to the director's door?

She jumped as Hammond Marsh spoke again.

"Are your volunteers ready to sail?" He resumed the conversation in a less angry tone. "I have authorized the captain of the *Belinda* to stand by for your orders. She can put into Monterey harbor and begin lading cargo as soon as you give the word."

Jenny clenched her fists in a gesture of sheer terror. In a moment they would be discussing the actual date of sailing — something that was intended to be kept a closely guarded secret! But if there was still someone in the hall to overhear —

She had to prevent that from happening!

Motioning Nadjia to remain still, Jenny straightened up and quickly crossed the room on tiptoe. It took every ounce of nerve she possessed to pull the door open wider and peer out. Then, abruptly, her tense body wilted in relief.

"You had me scared silly!" she scolded. "What are you *doing* out here?"

With folded arms and an expression that hinted at boredom, Van Gilbert was lounging nonchalantly against the corridor wall.

He glanced up in evident surprise at her question. "Waiting for my uncle, of course." He shrugged. "He told me to run along, but I know how impatient he can be at times. When he wants me, he wants me now. It's easier on his temper if I'm within call." Van eyed her curiously. "Why should my being here scare you?"

Feeling rather foolish, Jenny tried to explain. "Well, I didn't know it was *you!*" She pointed to the other room. "The walls are awfully thin. They were talking about sailing dates, and I —"

"Oh, I see. You figured it was Captain Kidd." Van grinned disarmingly. "As a matter of fact, the *Belinda*'s sailing will be about as hush-hush as the Rose Bowl Parade. Wait and see; every one of those volunteers will have at least twenty-six relatives on hand to wave good-bye to them.

They stampede down to the dock, shouting aloha, throwing confetti — The last secret sailing scored a rating of six on the seismograph's earthquake scale!"

Jenny was shaking with mirth at his description. "Shhh! They'll hear you!"

As if on cue, an irascible voice suddenly barked from the next room: "Van! You out there, boy? Come on in here, we need you."

"What did I tell you?" Van said *sotto voce.* He hurried out the door to answer the summons.

With her limited grasp of Hindi, Jenny could only try to explain to Nadjia that her fright of a few minutes earlier had been due to a misunderstanding.

"Nothing's wrong," she added with a smile. "You've been such a good girl to help me with these crates. Let's go see if your Daddy is back yet."

Nadjia followed her trustingly out into the corridor. As they passed Dr. Wynne's office Jenny heard Hammond Marsh expounding on his plans.

"I've decided to send the *Belinda* out at dusk — preferably under a thick cover of fog to shield her from those freebooters. What's the weather outlook for the next few days?"

The word "fog" had a chilling effect on Jenny's spirits. Apprehensively, she wondered if a heavy mist would cripple Mark's audacious scheme. Would it prevent his flares from being seen by the Coast Guard? Her heart contracted in fear at the thought of her brother swimming blindly around in the frigid Pacific. Fog could mean the difference between life and death for him.

"Australia? Oh, it's about nine thousand miles off in that direction." Jenny gestured vaguely at the limitless horizon. "Or maybe only six thousand; I can't remember. But a jet plane will whisk your father across all that ocean in no time. I imagine you can hardly wait to see him next month."

"That's for sure," Paul agreed.

For the past hour they had been sitting lazily on the damp sand at the water's edge. Every now and then, Jenny had noticed the boy darting a swift glance down the shoreline; he had been unusually quiet until she brought up the subject of his father's return.

His eyes turned in that direction again. This time there was a troubled frown on his face.

"The beach looks different without that old fence in the way," he commented. "If he had taken it down sooner, I wouldn't have had to swim around it those other times."

Jenny muffled a gasp. Perhaps the peaceful hour spent here by the water had jogged his memory!

"Or climb over it," she added as casually as she could. "I've often wondered why a smart boy like you would do such a silly thing."

Rather than shying away from the indirect question, Paul wrinkled his brow in an effort to remember.

"I'm positive there was a reason," he insisted. "Something funny I saw. Way down there. I wish I could think of what it was."

Jenny knew better than to try to press him. She leaned back on one elbow, absently tracing designs in the sand with the smooth edge of a shell. The day was beautifully sunny and warm, a sunbather's dream. Perfect for boating, too, she thought, noticing that a number of small craft were dotted along the ocean's glassy surface.

"It looks as if they are trawling out there. We ought to get a couple of fishing poles for ourselves," she remarked.

"I'd rather go whale-watching."

Paul's voice trailed off as he stared across the barely rippling breakers. Jenny followed his gaze. A sailboat, becalmed without a puff of air to inflate its sails, was temporarily stranded near a marker buoy.

"A whale would tip that one right over," she laughed.

But Paul had suddenly lost interest in fishing. He scrambled to his feet. "I — I think I'd better go in now, Jenny. I'm getting a sunburn."

She looked up at him in surprise. The tip of his nose was slightly pink, but it was his perturbed expression that troubled her most.

"What's the matter? Is that bump on your head starting to hurt again?"

"No, it's okay," he muttered. "Say, isn't Russ coming for dinner tonight? You'd better come in and get cleaned up, too."

Grabbing her towel and sunglasses, Jenny followed him across the sand. It wasn't like Paul to change the subject so abruptly, she thought. Just for a minute she wondered if he might have unexpectedly remembered the "something funny" he had seen on the beach so long ago. Then she smiled, hooting at her imagination. Surely he would have told her about it — wouldn't he?

In any case, she had little chance to ponder over Paul's odd behavior. She and Miss Ursula had planned a gala menu for Russ's farewell dinner, and there were still a number of last-minute dishes to be prepared.

Everything was ready by the time he arrived at six o'clock. Jenny had changed into her prettiest dress, a full-skirted cotton of the palest blue, and had brushed her short black hair until it glistened. The appreciative look Russ gave her was more than enough reward for her pains.

When the sumptuous meal was finished, he complimented the two chefs on their culinary artistry. He seemed especially pleased by the cake they had baked and had decorated with a tiny steamship and the words "bon voyage."

"I said good-bye to Deedee at the Center this morning," Jenny told him after dinner as they walked outside for a last stroll together in the garden. "She's been a dear friend. I'll miss her — and you too, Russ."

"Will you? I'm glad." He paused to gaze wistfully down at her. "I can't imagine how I'll be able to keep my mind on my work, knowing that you are half a world away from me."

"I'll write. Airmail. As often as you like," Jenny promised softly.

"Six times a day?" Russ gathered her in his arms. "I knew all along that this was no time to fall in love. But I couldn't help myself. Will you marry me, Jenny? In two years — or sooner if I can get home on leave?"

Jenny's eyes filled with tears that were both happy and sad. But there was only joy in her reply.

She lifted her face to his. "Oh, yes, Russ. Whenever you say!"

A few minutes later, they reluctantly started back to the house. "I wish I could come down and see you off," Jenny said, holding tightly to his hand. "But I understand that Dr. Wynne has put a stop to visitors cluttering up the dock."

"Yes, it's just another precaution," Russ explained. "He and Mr. Marsh had even hoped to hide our ship in a fogbank, but the *Belinda* has been here a week and the weather simply won't cooperate. I'm not sorry, though. I keep thinking of your brother, and the job he has to do out there tonight."

"Me too. I haven't heard from Mark in

ages. I — I'll be praying that you both come through safely."

Jenny bit her lip, determined not to cry. Not until he had gone, anyway. But her eyes were suspiciously bright as she watched Miss Ursula give him a fond kiss and Paul hold out his hand for a manly shake.

Russ had sold his car a few days earlier, and Dr. Avery offered to drive him down to the dock. "I'll be staying on at the Center afterward," the professor added. "Dr. Wynne has asked his entire staff to remain together until the *Belinda* is well out to sea."

Remembering the angry discussion she had overheard, Jenny guessed at the reason for the director's request. He was determined to prove to Mr. Marsh that no one connected with the Center was involved in the hijackings.

She waved to Russ and again wished him a pleasant journey. Their real good-bye, though, had been said in the garden. That was the farewell she would cling to during their long separation, Jenny thought sadly as the car's taillights faded into rosy blurs at the foot of the hill.

She was almost glad to tackle the huge stack of dirty dishes awaiting her in the kitchen. Maybe if she could stay busy enough, she would forget to worry.

The ruse didn't work, however. By the time the counters were scrubbed and the last plate set in the cupboard, Jenny's anxiety had increased to a fever pitch. There would be no peace of mind for her until Mark was safely back on dry land — and the *Belinda*'s passengers through the danger zone unscathed!

As was her habit, Miss Ursula retired early. Jenny managed to conceal her nervousness until the elderly lady had gone upstairs, but Paul saw through the pretense.

"Russ is your special friend, isn't he? Are you afraid the pirates might get him?" he asked.

Jenny had been watching the last wisps of daylight fade from the sky. Dusk — and then darkness. The *Belinda* would be sailing soon, now, before the moon rose to spotlight her location.

"Yes, Russ is my very special friend," she answered gently. "And I'm worried about — well, about a lot of things. About him, and the pirates, and about someone else who is awfully dear to me."

"That's what I thought," Paul gulped. He shifted uncomfortably from one foot to the other. "Listen, Jenny, I've got to tell you something. I went outside a little while ago, and there were voices — whispers, sort of — down on the beach."

The Briswalds taking a nocturnal stroll, Jenny surmised. But — whispers?

"It was probably our neighbors out for a walk," she said calmly.

"No. There's something else, too. All of a sudden this afternoon I remembered," Paul went on doggedly. "About why the bad man chased me. He was mad because of what I saw. It was a boat — a great big boat!"

# Chapter Sixteen

The implications of what Paul was trying to tell her struck Jenny with sledgehammer force.

"A great big boat?" She stared numbly into his guileless brown eyes. "Honey, this could be terrifically important. How big?"

"A whopper! I only got a peek at it. But it was lots taller than me," he added quickly. "I know, because I started to walk up onto the beach to get a better look at that funny long thing sticking off the front of it. That's when the bad man started yelling. You should have seen how fast I swam back here that day!"

"Oh, good Lord!"

To Jenny's horrified mind, his childish description sounded ominously familiar. "A speedy cutter" Elaine had called the pirates' craft. And others had remarked on the boat's size, and emphasized that it was heavily armed. Undoubtedly, the "funny long thing" Paul had glimpsed was a gun!

So Mark's superiors had been right, she thought, and her own hunch that Mr.

Briswald was only a victim of circumstantial evidence seemed completely wrong. A tremendous surge of relief washed over her. How lucky that the Coast Guard had been forewarned. They must be out there now, waiting for the gunboat to leave the snugness of its harbor!

She darted to the window, peering searchingly out at the impenetrable darkness. Sky and ocean merged together into a single murky element. Nowhere could she see even a pinpoint of light, no luminous circle of moon, not even a winking star to relieve the utter blackness of the night. And on the sea itself there was no sign of a ship standing guard over the coastline.

Jenny's heart gave a sickening lurch. Where was the Navy? Why weren't they rendezvousing now to protect the *Belinda* — and Mark?

"Paul, we — we can't just stand here." Her voice emerged in a petrified croak. "We've got to do something to help!"

He moved quickly to the wall phone. "Shall I call the police? They'll come. They'll put the bad man in jail, where he can't chase me any more!"

Something in his shrill, excited voice made Jenny pause. Supposing, just supposing, that Paul were exaggerating this thing all out of proportion? Not for a minute did she doubt that he had seen a boat — but, glimpsed with his frightened eyes, it might have loomed larger than life in his imagination. And the "long funny thing" — couldn't it have been a fishing rod mounted on the vessel's stern, rather than a gun?

Another dampening thought occurred to her. Paul had made it sound as if the boat were concealed nearby. Yet she herself had scrutinized every inch of the Briswalds' property. There was simply no way for the former sea captain to have hidden a craft of any size above the shallow inlet that bounded his yard

"Wait a minute, hon. I think we had better make sure of what you saw before we call out the Marines."

Paul's face drooped with disappointment. "But Jenny — the pirates! They might get away. Don't you believe me?"

"I believe you saw something. All sorts of people around here own boats, though." She lifted her old navy blue coat off a hook and then helped him into a hooded jacket that would hide his bright hair.

"Come on." She smiled reassuringly at him. "We'll hike down and take another peek at this ocean liner you found. Then if anything looks the least bit peculiar about it, we can run back here and call all the police you want."

"All right. But hurry! I'll bet they were only standing around talking while they waited for the whole gang to show up."

His confident prediction sent Jenny scrambling for a pair of walking shoes. Pulling the kitchen door noiselessly shut behind her, she saw his hurrying form already halfway down the path to the gate.

Gradually her eyes adjusted to the intense darkness. "Wait, Paul," she called softly as she rounded the stone wall, which blotted out the lights of the house.

He hesitated impatiently for a few seconds while she caught up, then scurried ahead again. Ordinarily when they were together it was she who took the lead, but this time he moved forward determinedly, keen on proving that he had been telling the truth.

Sand sifted into Jenny's shoes, and a chunk of driftwood snatched at her ankles as she stumbled along the beach. Aware that sound traveled clearly and for long distances across the water, she fought down a squeak of fright and hurried on.

The sea moaned and sighed just off to her right, a lost, forlorn sound that only increased Jenny's growing edginess. Looking up, she saw a hulking shadow, darker even than the black sky above. The Briswalds' home, she realized, swallowing hard. And still no sign of a boat. Where was Paul taking her?

She forged ahead as quickly as possible, keeping her eyes glued on the small hastening figure in front of her. Although he outdistanced her by only a few yards, it was difficult to keep him in sight. His dark clothing was all but invisible against the black mass of the cliff. For an instant she lost sight of him altogether and had to restrain the impulse to shout his name.

The soft lapping of water dead ahead halted her. Jenny peered down and found herself standing alongside the tiny inlet that channeled across the sand at the far boundary of their neighbors' property. Now what? she wondered.

Suddenly Paul was at her side, tugging her hand. "There's a narrow spot up that way. We can jump across without getting wet," he whispered.

Jenny stood her ground, unwilling to trespass any farther. "Why should we cross the stream? There's no boat here."

"I know that, silly. This is way too shallow," he said impatiently. "We have to go around the ledge to the other side of the cliff. The cove there is plenty deep, and it runs clear in underneath the mountain."

"The other side of the cliff! But that's Mr. Marsh's land," she exclaimed. "The 'bad man' lives *here*, right next to us!"

In the gloom she could see Paul's face whirl upward in astonishment. "You mean Mr. Briswald? Honest, Jenny, he's all right once you get to know him." He clutched her hand and pulled her up the slope to the narrowest tongue of the inlet. Hopping easily across, he beckoned for her to do the same.

In complete bewilderment Jenny followed his lead. But when she had cleared the water and was standing in the shadow of the cliff, she grabbed Paul's shoulder and demanded an explanation.

"Look here, young man, this has gone far enough! I haven't seen a single thing tonight that looks suspicious, except the way you've been acting. If Mr. Briswald isn't your 'bad man,' who is?"

"I — I don't know his name, exactly," Paul stammered.

Jenny had a number of sharp comments to make about wild-goose chases. But before even one angry word could leave her lips, a puff of wind wafted their way, bringing with it the distinct if muted rumble of mens' voices.

To Jenny, a blizzardy wind could have been no more chilling. She bit her lip, hardly aware that she and Paul had frozen in position like a pair of landlocked icebergs. The breeze had sprung up out of the west, and it carried an eerie murmur of half-distinct noises through the clear night air.

The faint crunch of feet on the crisp, dry sand. A cough that ended in a muffled sneeze. The merest snatch of conversation — "catch her easy; no strain" — and a boisterous guffaw cut suddenly short.

"See? I'd have told you about him this afternoon, only I didn't want to hurt your feelings." Paul mouthed the words in her ear. "I thought you liked him a lot. Then tonight when Russ came, I found out *he* was your special boy friend. It's okay, isn't it, Jenny? You aren't mad at me any more?"

Jenny scarcely heard him. Even now she found it difficult to believe the appalling truth. Still, she thought, coming slowly back to life, this discovery clarified so many things — things that had puzzled her in the past.

She knew now where the pirates had obtained their precise information. And why the Center's ships, and only theirs, had been attacked. The knowledge was almost blindingly clear.

She looked down and saw that Paul was still waiting anxiously for her answer. "Sure, it's okay," she gulped. "I'm sorry, hon. I've been pretty thickheaded, haven't I?"

She stared apprehensively, at the slim ledge that wound around the base of the cliff. "Would it be safe to slip across there and try to get a look at their boat? I want to be absolutely sure —"

This time it was Paul who hung back. "I guess it would be easy enough," he conceded reluctantly.

His zest for adventure had suddenly vanished, Jenny realized. She stooped down and whispered instructions to him.

"I'll go first. You stay behind me. If they should see me — if anything happens — turn around *quietly* and run for help as fast as you can. Agreed?"

He nodded. Jenny tugged her coat collar up around her face as far as it would go, then began inching soundlessly along the rim of the hillside until she reached the slender isthmus that formed a narrow walkway along its outer perimeter. Her heart pounded in her chest like a jungle tom-tom beating out a warning.

*Go back! Go back! Go back!* it seemed to throb.

But Jenny knew that to flee now would be cowardly. One glimpse of the hidden cove and what must lie within it would dispel every last lingering doubt. Even if the Coast Guard vessels weren't lying in wait somewhere out on that black ocean, even if her brother had failed to gain the confidence of the buccaneers, she would know. And she would testify, shout the truth to the world. Not all the courage in the Sheldon family belonged to Mark!

Her foot encountered a gnarled tentacle of root looping snakelike out from the cliff's rugged exterior. Jenny stepped cautiously over it and felt the stony bulge at her side suddenly curve inward.

Far above on the precipice perched the mansion of Hammond Marsh. Tons of solid rock supported the house, lifting it much higher above sea level than the homes of any of his neighbors. In the gloom of night, without a glimmer of light to soften its windows, it seemed a brooding, almost foreboding place.

Her gaze dropped, skipped across the half-crescent of beach beyond the tiny bay, and came to rest on the cove itself. Not so much as a stray leaf marred its faintly shimmering surface.

Empty!

But the triangle of sand between cliff and cove most decidedly was not. Half a dozen shadowy figures waited there, their faceless forms turned away from her and focused on the blank steeply rising mountain of rock beneath the house.

Her straining ears caught the mutter of a rasping voice.

"Get ready. The boss is bringing her out now."

Jenny shrank back against the cliff, trying to make herself as inconspicuous as possible. Bringing who out? And where was their boat?

A creaking rumble from the mountainside provided the answer to both questions. What she had assumed to be solid rock took the shape of a massive door. Inch by inch, it swung spookily open to reveal the hull of a small powerful ship. Small in tonnage, but not in might. Mounted on its foredeck was a long, hollow shape. Not a gun, Jenny thought dazedly. A cannon!

A faint throb of engines hummed and pulsed as the ghost-gray vessel edged out into the cove.

Almost forgetting her terror, Jenny stared dumbfounded at the enormous gap. How diabolically clever! The door had been built and carefully painted to camouflage a mammoth cave beneath the hillside.

No wonder the cutter had been termed a phantom ship! No wonder the most minute search had never succeeded in locating it!

Far back in the yawning cave, a flutter of white caught Jenny's eye. The graceful outlines of a sailboat bobbed gently in the cutter's wake. She understood now how Paul had come to glimpse the larger vessel. The door must have been opened so that the *Hurricane Edna* could be floated out. Its owner would have taken precautions, of course, to make sure that no ships were in the vicinity to spot his actions. It was only his bad luck that the boy happened to be out for a forbidden swim that day.

At that instant, bad luck overtook Jenny as well.

Her coat sleeve had been straining more and more tightly against the face of the cliff as she crouched tensely in its shadow. She had not noticed the few particles of soil sifting down upon her as the increasing pressure forced them out. Only when a large rock was dislodged from its claylike bed, yards above her head, did she realize the danger.

She heard it start to roll downward. Taking an automatic step backward, she thrust out her hands to try to catch the stone. But she wasn't quick enough. It tumbled recklessly down the slope, landing on the ledge with a dull thud before bouncing into the water.

The telltale splash alerted the pirate crew just as they were in the act of climbing aboard the cutter. To a man they swung around, staring with hard, suspicious faces at the spot where she stood hidden.

From behind her came a faint frightened gasp. "Get out of here. Scoot!" Jenny hissed at Paul.

He hesitated for no more than a split second before melting away into the darkness. Half a breath later, Jenny heard the muffled "plop" of feet landing hard on the sand, and breathed a thankful prayer that he had safely leaped the inlet. Hastily she scampered back along the ledge, trying to put distance between herself and the hijackers now that Paul had eluded them.

But time had run out.

Brawny hands seized her wrists, and fingers like steel locked over her mouth, cutting off her scream for help. A moment later, she was rudely thrust into the center of a glowering circle of men.

"We got us a spy, Captain. What say we feed her to the fishes?" her captor bluntly suggested.

Still struggling for her life, Jenny had no chance to identify any of their faces until the man addressed as "Captain" stepped boldly forward.

"That wasn't very bright, Jenny," said Van Gilbert softly. "That wasn't very bright at all."

Menace colored every inflection of his voice, rendering the words far more sinister than any actual threat could have done. Staring wide-eyed up at him, Jenny wondered how she could ever have considered Van handsome. His dark sneering features and swooping brows now resembled a mask — a mask of pure evil!

He couldn't afford to let her go, she realized. Not now. Not ever. An appeal to him on the grounds of their former friendship would be futile. Nor would it accomplish anything to shriek that there had been another witness. At best, he would ignore her. At the worst — Jenny shuddered, thinking of Paul's fate at the hands of this ruthless man.

A leering sailor who somehow seemed vaguely familiar stepped forward, brandishing a gun. Jenny swallowed hard, remembering where she had last seen him. His face had been half obscured by fog that day on the dock, but there was no mistaking that vicious expression.

"Want me to take care of her?" he asked. " 'Twouldn't be no trouble —"

Van intercepted his motion. "Put that away, you clod! Want to have the whole seacoast swarming with cops?"

He pivoted around slowly, assessing the uneasy circle of men surrounding him. Suddenly a grin broke over his taut features.

"I believe we'll let the newest member of our crew prove his mettle," he said. "This is our last raid, and if we pull it off we'll be away scot-free, each with a tidy nest egg. So don't make any mistakes!"

A dark figure shambled forward, a man who looked no less evil than his companions. "Flood tide's on the turn," he said laconically. "Might be best if she drowned — accidental-like. It happens, to folks who get careless. And that way there'll be no questions asked later."

Wrenching her away from the man who still pinioned her arms, he clamped a hand across Jenny's lips and dragged her mercilessly over to the water's edge.

"Don't try to yell," he advised, and mouthed two more almost inaudible words, which she alone could hear.

Then something hard whistled down on her skull. Jenny felt herself plunging backwards — falling, falling into the icy depths of the outrushing tide.

# Chapter Seventeen

It was an effort not to battle the current, to keep her body limp and lifeless-appearing while the gushing tide rocketed her out toward the open sea. But Mark's whispered advice, "Play dead!" echoed like a grim life-or-death warning in Jenny's ears.

The heavy butt of his revolver had barely grazed her skull, so she was still fully conscious when she pitched backwards into the water. One floundering motion, though, would put a sudden gruesome end to her reprieve.

Fortunately, once she had been carried a few yards from the shore, the inky blackness of the night concealed her movements from Van and his crew. Luck was on her side, too, in that they had little time to spare. It must have taken only seconds to convince them that she was dead — or soon would be.

Underneath the water the gunboat's engines roared with a renewed pulse. The ghost-gray vessel rapidly gathered speed as it churned seaward. Jenny took several frantic strokes to get out of its path, then gulped a deep breath of air and buried her face in the water.

Only when its seething wake had foamed past did she dare raise her head. Not so much as a flaring match illuminated the boat's shadowy hulk. Its very darkness frightened her anew. So many lives were jeopardized by the evil men aboard.

At that moment, however, a more immediate fear gripped Jenny. Her sodden coat was increasing in weight every second, its leaden bulk threatening to drag her to the bottom. Treading water, she tore at the buttons and at last struggled free of the encumbrance.

Even then it was no easy matter to regain the safety of the shore. The current was a terrifyingly powerful force that sucked the strength from her legs and tugged with liquid tentacles at her thrashing arms. For endlessly long minutes she battled toward the dim coastline, losing a stroke for every two that carried her ahead.

Jenny was thoroughly winded by the time her feet touched bottom. Gasping for breath, she staggered through the last few yards of shallow water and collapsed onto the oozing sand.

She had no recollection of blacking out,

but she remembered nothing further until Paul's feverishly anxious voice aroused her.

"She's dead! They've drowned her!" he sobbed.

"No, lad. She's coming around now," a second, gruffer voice soothed him.

Jenny opened her eyes to see Mr. Briswald kneeling beside her. He helped her sit up, then stripped off his own jacket and wrapped it around her trembling shoulders.

"You've had a bad time of it, miss, but you're safe now," he said kindly. "Those brigands must not have reckoned on your being such a strong swimmer."

Jenny managed a feeble smile. "One of them did. My brother also knew there would be little chance for me on shore. That's why he pretended to let me drown."

She struggled to her feet. "Oh, my gosh! Mark! Quick, call the Coast Guard," she begged. "They must get ships out there to help him!"

"We did that first thing," Paul said proudly. "Mr. Briswald phoned them, and he phoned the police and he phoned the Harbor Patrol — and then we came back to look for you. Only you weren't here, and I — I was afraid —"

"Those villains had already put out to sea when we arrived," their neighbor added. "They won't get far this time, however. The ocean is swarming with ships waiting to intercept them. Apparently, our warning wasn't needed."

With a sigh of relief, Jenny turned back to the whitecapped sea. So everything had gone according to plan, after all. With one important difference. It would be Van, not the former sea captain, who would fall into their trap. She realized now that the naval vessels must have doused their lights in hopes of luring the hijackers out from shore.

"I guess we were very foolish —" she began, but Paul interrupted her with a shriek of excitement.

"Jenny, look! Something's happening out there!"

She gasped in shock as an explosive burst of whitehot flame brightened the distant horizon. As if some master magician had flipped a switch, small bright lights popped on all over the ocean. A dozen or more ships rapidly began converging on the point where the first brilliant burst had appeared.

A cold, numb sensation crept over Jenny. The Coast Guard was closing in on Van and his crew, but what of Mark? He was supposed to have sent up flares! Yet, no red signal beacon had arced through the night skies — only that single hideous volley, which had sounded like the report of a cannon.

She kept staring at the ocean until her eyes burned from the strain. It was impossible to tell what was taking place out there, but she couldn't force herself to look away. What if the gunshot had shattered the *Belinda*'s hull? What if Mark had been overpowered —

Suddenly a firm hand clasped her arm, and a no-nonsense voice said crisply, "Amos, have you lost your senses? What can you be thinking of, letting this poor girl stand here freezing to death?"

Martha Briswald steered Jenny away from the water's edge and up the terraced slope. A pinch of color had been added to her worn face, and her voice was no longer drab and resigned.

"The police arrived a few minutes ago," she declared. "They brought along the Center's staff, and a force of Harbor officials as well. I'm afraid you and this young man are in for a siege of questioning."

Jenny was surprised to find Miss Ursula waiting for them at the kitchen door.

Although she had recently been awakened from a sound sleep, she bustled around more actively than some people half her age, alternately scolding and lavishing affection on both her adventurous charges.

"Dear me, such a tumult this has caused!" she exclaimed. "Sit down for a minute, Paul. Jenny, run upstairs and get right out of those soaking clothes. I'll find Clement and have him help me make sandwiches for that throng in the living room."

"No, please. Let me help," offered Mrs. Briswald.

By the time Jenny had changed into dry clothing, the two ladies were acting like old friends, and hot coffee, along with heaping trays of sandwiches and cookies, was being distributed among the hungry men.

A cup of the scalding brew made Jenny feel considerably better, too, though she was still desperately worried about Mark and her friends aboard the *Belinda*. Responding to a barrage of questions, she patiently described the daring masquerade her brother had used to hoodwink the pirates. Then she and Paul gave an account of what had happened in the cove.

"Paul was smarter than I," she admitted ruefully. "He tumbled to the fact that Van was a 'bad man' ages ago. It never occurred to me to suspect him until tonight."

She cast a sheepish glance at Mr. Briswald. "I guess I should have, but I got sidetracked by a red herring. Van certainly had the most logical motive of all for attacking those ships. As Hammond Marsh's only relative, he stood to inherit a fortune someday — but Van must have been afraid that if Mr. Marsh kept pouring money into the Center, there wouldn't be any fortune left to inherit!"

"It's hard to believe." Dr. Wynne shook his head. "To think that anyone could be so greedy —"

"May we join the discussion?" asked a new voice from the doorway.

Everyone whirled to stare at the young man attired in a smart Navy uniform who had suddenly appeared in their midst. Everyone but Jenny, that is. One look at him and the second youth waiting by the door was enough to send her flying across the room.

"Mark! Russ!" she cried, trying to embrace them both simultaneously. "Thank heavens you're safe! But — but why —"

"Why aren't I on my way to India?" Russ

interpreted her bewildered stammer. "The *Belinda* had a slight mishap. It will take a couple of weeks to make her seaworthy again."

Mark chuckled. "Longer than that to refloat Van Gilbert's cutter, I'm afraid. One of his crewmen got overeager when the *Belinda*'s skipper wouldn't heed their command to halt. He tried to cut across her bow — and wound up ramming her. A keg of powder on the cutter's deck was detonated by the force of the collision. We all had to jump for it. Fortunately, the Coast Guard was nearby to fish us out of the drink, and the last of the buccaneers are now in the brig."

"They should be made to walk the plank," Mr. Briswald grumbled. "That collision — it sounds a great deal like the tragedy that befell my own ship."

"It was similar in more ways than one, Captain Bohling," Mark nodded, using the man's correct name. "The same inept helmsman was responsible for both incidents. Earlier this evening he had been boasting about the way he and his cohorts had placed the blame on you at the trial, and their confession is now down on paper. I am sure the Maritime Board will move to have you exonerated and reinstated to your former position immediately."

At this splendid piece of news, Captain Bohling straightened his shoulders and joyfully clasped his wife's hand.

"For months I have been working to get at the truth of the matter," he said. "I even changed my name and followed those men to California when they were transferred from the East Coast. Detectives whom I hired reported that they frequently visited the Marsh residence, so I rented the house next door."

Amos Bohling glanced again at his wife. "This watching and waiting has been especially hard on Martha. After what happened back East, I wanted to turn my back on the whole human race. I built that fence, and we kept to ourselves. My only goal was to catch those men in some other nefarious act. I knew that somehow I had to prove that their word couldn't be trusted."

"Oh! So that is why you spent so much time staring out at the ocean!" Jenny exclaimed.

"Yes, although I succeeded in learning nothing useful that way," Captain Bohling admitted. "I did spot a cabin cruiser approaching the beach one night, but it had disappeared before I could get down to the cliff. No doubt that scurvy crew was picking up their chief for a secret meeting."

"Those men were blackmailed into participating in the pirate raids," Mark explained. "Somehow Van Gilbert discovered that they had been responsible for the sinkings of the *Yankee Trader* and the *Nantucket.* He threatened to expose them unless they helped him carry out his own scheme. Van knew how much the ships of the Marsh Line meant to his uncle. He figured that by attacking them he could undermine the old man's trust in the Center."

"And he nearly succeeded!" Dr. Avery gasped. "Hammond threatened to withdraw his support from the organization if one more cargo was hijacked."

"Yes, just last week he warned me that that was his intention," the director sighed. "Come to think of it, Van must have been listening at the door that day. No doubt what he overheard made him all the more determined to stop the *Belinda!*"

"Well, it's over now. He'll have no chance to plan any more dirty work from behind bars," Mark assured the group. "Oddly enough, he didn't know your true identity, Captain Bohling. But he had noticed you using that spyglass, and he decided that you would make a good decoy. It was he who started the rumors that you were involved in the piracy. I'm sorry to say that for a time we believed him."

"Van's courage vanished after that dunking he took tonight, though. He has confessed fully and has even named the man who handled the transshipment of the cargoes to Red China. He considered it an ironic joke to hand the goods over to the Center's enemies — for a fat profit, of course."

The questions went on for hours afterward. Paul fell asleep in his chair and was carried upstairs by his grandfather. Delight at having both her brother and her fiancé safely back with her kept Jenny alert for a while longer, but gradually her eyelids, too, began drooping.

"Sis, you'd better get some sleep before you keel over in that chair," Mark advised. "You must be bushed after that long swim home. Is your head all right? I didn't hurt you, did I?"

"Not really. But I certainly got wet!" she laughed.

"To tell the truth, I was about ready to

start aiming my gun at Van's crewmen," he confessed. "Then when they chose me to 'dispose' of you, I saw a way to get you safely out of there and still keep in good standing with those cutthroats. It was important that I stay with them as long as possible," he added. "We didn't have any solid evidence against them until they actually hailed the *Belinda.*"

Jenny shivered when she thought of how differently the evening could have ended. But miraculously, everything had turned out well. "Will I see you again before you rejoin your ship?" she asked.

"Of course. I'm slated to be the star witness at their trial," he assured her. "*Now* will you go to bed?"

Russ held out his hand. "I'll walk you to the stairs." He did so, and gave her a quick kiss good night. "See you in the morning," he promised. "Not bright and early, though. I have something to talk over with Dr. Wynne first."

It was mid-afternoon before he returned. By then, Jenny had enjoyed a luxurious ten-hour sleep and had read half a dozen different newspaper accounts of the dramatic climax to last evening's excitement. Each article ran a four-column photo of Mark, who was described as the Navy's "daring undercover agent responsible for scuttling the plans of a modern-day band of pirates."

"I had forgotten that Van once served in the Coast Guard," Jenny remarked to Russ. "No wonder he knew just how to handle that cutter!"

"Lucky for us that his helmsman wasn't equally adept." He grinned, and took the newspaper away from her and tossed it over his shoulder. "Let's forget those crooks and talk about something more important. Do you remember my proposing to you, Miss Sheldon?"

"Well, of course! It was only yesterday."

"Was it? Seems like that all happened centuries ago. Anyway, I've changed my mind." Russ smiled teasingly, and continued before she could speak. "About waiting two years, that is. Jenny, I couldn't stand being away from you that long. Will you marry me now — this week — and come with me to India?"

"Oh, Russ!" Jenny could only stare at him in amazement. "But — the Center?"

"You're being shanghaied! They absolutely insist on adding you to their roster of volunteers." Russ paused, looking wistful. "The final answer is up to you, though. Will you come?"

Only a few short months earlier, Jenny had been worrying about a career. Now she knew she had found her lifework. She nodded joyfully and held out her arms to him.

"Yes, darling. To India — to the ends of the earth. I'll come!"

We hope you have enjoyed this Large Print book. Other G.K. Hall & Co. or Chivers Press Large Print books are available at your library or directly from the publishers.

For more information about current and upcoming titles, please call or write, without obligation, to:

G.K. Hall & Co.
P.O. Box 159
Thorndike, Maine 04986 USA
Tel. (800) 223-1244
        (800) 223-6121
OR

Chivers Press Limited
Windsor Bridge Road
Bath BA2 3AX
England
Tel. (0225) 335336

All our Large Print titles are designed for easy reading, and all our books are made to last.